FOUND AND LOST

Found and Lost
Edited & Compiled by
Rohan P. Lapalikar

Paperback Edition

First published in India in 2023 by

Inkfeathers Publishing
Vivek Vihar, New Delhi 110095
www.inkfeathers.com

ISBN 978-93-90882-96-0

FOUND AND LOST

Edited & Compiled by

Rohan P. Lapalikar

Inkfeathers Publishing
www.inkfeathers.com

Disclaimer

The anthology "Found and Lost" is a collection of 23 short stories written by 18 authors who belong to different parts of the world.

Unless otherwise indicated, all the names, characters, objects, businesses, places, events, incidents—whether physical/non-physical, real/unreal, tangible/ intangible in whatsoever description used in this book are either the product of the author's imagination or used in a fictitious manner. Any resemblance to actual persons, objects, entities, living or dead, or actual events is purely coincidental.

The contents published in this book are solely owned by their respective authors and are in no way intended to hurt anyone's religious, political, spiritual, brand, personal or fanatic beliefs and/or faith, whatsoever. In case, any sort of plagiarism is detected in the contents within this anthology or in case of any complaints, grievances, or objections, neither the anthology editor nor the publisher is to be held responsible.

Curated with the writings of

Vanshika Gupta, Varun Sargwan, Nadeem Shah, Shay P. Kris,

Dr. Sanjana Venkatraman, Shelina Rajawat, Mahek Thakar,

Vanitha Murugan, Surya Sai Prasanth Palaparthy,

Ishat Sharma, Chandni Ahuja, Prerna Dhingra,

Aniket Gauns, Esther Graciya. G, Naina Khemani,

Vijila M, Upasana Hembram, Rohan P. Lapalikar

Contents

About the Editor

Rohan P. Lapalikar hails from Mumbai, whose life revolves around his family. He is a teacher by profession, also a comic, and a passionate photographer by hobby. He loves writing fictional stories and poems. He believes that 'The universe is made up of not just Atoms and Molecules, but also stories and poetry.' He feels an eternal connection with nature, along with a little blend of soft music. He is a compassionate animal lover as well. He loves to be full of life and try out new ventures. Found and Lost is his first anthology as an editor. He wishes to pursue further studies in infection biology in the United Kingdom and work as a research scientist. He goes by the pen name–Moony.

Preface

Remember as a kid, we used to have a department in our school named, Lost and Found, and every time we lost our belongings, we seek them there. Well, "Found and Lost" as the title implies is quite the opposite of that.

One day as I sipped a hot cup of coffee sitting on the porch outside my home, a friend, Kedar, asked me to break the silence, 'Why do you seem so lost? Are you okay?'

And hastily I replied, 'I think I lost Naina.'

Amongst the two most important chapters of my life, which made me who I am today, Naina, the one with the most beautiful eyes, was one of them. I met her on a solo trip to Himachal Pradesh in December 2017. She was a simple girl, not the type of girl any random guy would want, but the one who I needed. Her voice echoes in me to date. That trip paved the path for our future. We were together, for 2 years after she proposed to me on my birthday in 2018. Until the Covid-19 pandemic hit, WE became history in my mind. I never heard her voice since. Never saw her smile, and never could I love anyone completely as much as I loved her. Perhaps, I will, in the future.

We all have been in love, right? Once, twice, or more than that.

In recent times, or long ago. Be it a friend, girlfriend, boyfriend, animal, someone of the same caste, someone from another caste, or all of them at the same time. I still remember how it felt when I loved someone for the first-time decades ago. It was not like how the Bollywood films show, but it wasn't any different either. Those days were all about her. Naiveness was at its peak. I imagined that's how love is supposed to be. You love, propose, stay with each other, get married, and grow old. As puberty hit, I realized love happens at a cost. And the price is pain, suffering, damage, to lose yourself.

Well, the question that Kedar asked me, was the seed that gave birth to the concept of this anthology. I wondered if there are any more stories like this one, where the love never achieved its fate and stayed incomplete. Of course, there were, I just had to search for them.

I was always an emotional guy, who felt too much, expressed too much, observed too much, loved so much, and then landed into suffering. Little did I know in my early days, the ability to feel is a gift more than a curse. I believed in eternal love, where your destiny tests you and pushes you off-limits. And if you pass, God himself bends the rules. I used to think that being sensitive and emotional is the root of all suffering until I looked inside me and realized that my weakness according to the cruel world out there is my greatest strength after all.

This brings me to the second most loved chapter of my life, Lucas.

God made us cross paths while I was en route to my college, and he was lying under the car with a wounded back. That cute little Indian pariah pup with blue eyes wagged his tail and cried for help with teary eyes. So, I bunked my college and got him treated, kept him at me for a week till the wound heals. But that one week, I must say I was not the one prior. And then, a loving family adopted him.

Isn't it strange, that some people love you, and some people are a lesson? And then there are some, who teach you how to love, before leaving.

With this in my mind, I came up with the theme of this anthology, and voila! It got accepted and I present you, Found and Lost, Tales of an incomplete love.

This book is for everyone who seeks hope and love, for everyone who carries the grief of dead feelings, for everyone who has lost someone despite pure intentions and heart, and for everyone who suffered pain that you never deserved. To you my dear Reader, I open my heart.

Feliz lectura!

1

One More Time

Dr. Sanjana Venkatraman

Creaaaaak

The heavy dark brown wooden door of my school classroom creaked open as my frail hands struggled to push it towards the room. I dodged a beam of fresh white sunlight from cutting through my body like the cockroach dodged my scalpel yesterday in anatomy class. I caught my breath back as it entered my lungs and I felt embarrassment seep into my face.

I was all of 5 minutes late to my math class but felt guilty and embarrassed like I was caught murdering someone. Not that I have or ever want to, but my expressions would easily expose me. I walked through my classroom to my seat as eyeballs pierced my skin.

*****

As I frantically brushed my dog Buddy's hair off of me, I felt Riya's hands patting my shoulder and I turned around to witness her usual smirk. I called Buddy "my" dog even though he wasn't allowed into our home.

I frowned slightly and turned back only to be welcomed by my angry mother.

'How many times should I tell you to not go around with that dog?' she shouted. She disliked me even hanging out with dogs as my asthma flared up.

'God! Mom c'mon,' I sighed.

Riya stepped forward and hugged Mom as I walked into my room. Riya was always the peacemaker. She wasn't into arguments and would do everything she could to avoid conflict, I, on the other hand, would dive head-first into it.

I had known Riya for 12 years of my life and couldn't imagine life without her. We shared every little detail of our days with each other. Her father worked in the Navy and was away for most of her childhood. She lost her mother to Leptospirosis, back when our society was a Rat-house. Her grandmother, Nani, lived with her and almost entirely brought her up. Most people mistook Nani for Riya's mother. Her jet-black hair and immense stamina must've contributed to this assumption.

Riya and I had been on many fun adventures together and it was something that brought out the explorative and fun side in her. Otherwise, she was always quiet and kept to herself.

We spent the entire day packing our bags for our school trip which was scheduled for the next day. It was THIS, ONE TRIP we were waiting for our entire lives, well, the school lives precisely. We were going outside the city for the first time together! Even though the city was only 2 hours away, the excitement was overwhelming.

SLURP

I opened my eyes to a humongous but gorgeous face staring down at me with anticipation, right up into my soul. There was a freaking dog in my room.

For a moment, I felt shivers rush through my spinal column. I saw a faint figure behind Buddy and my heart raced.

'Did my mom know?' I wondered.

I heard a familiar voice. 'HAPPY BIRTHDAY!' said Riya in her happy yet calm and soothing voice.

It was my 15th birthday on the day of our school trip, and it felt like the best of everything was happening to me. Buddy was the cutest little bundle of grey fur when we first saw him on the streets in Mumbai. His ears were very tender and fell over his face, partially covering his eyes. Riya and I found him a couple of weeks ago. Every single day, we would meet him, regardless of what is happening in our lives. In my defense, he was not like the other dogs. There was just something different about him, his eyes spoke.

When his jet-black eyes looked into yours, you could feel his soul communicating with you. There was an entire universe in there that nobody knew of. Nobody, other than the two of us.

I patiently waited for Buddy to implant kisses all over my face before I pushed my body out of the bed.

'How much longer?' I asked.

'Till we leave?' said Riya.

'No, till my mom finds out her worst nightmare has come true!' I spoke.

On the day of my birthday, Riya had sneaked our little Buddy into my house as a surprise gift for me. But I was certain it was going to take a deadly turn. Riya was the kind of friend who'd make all your desires come true for you. She would go out of her way to perform acts of kindness. It is no surprise that her good heart was my favorite part of her.

Now that we had to leave for the school bus, it hit us like a ton of bricks.

'What were we going to do with Buddy?' We both gave a thought.

Without a second thought or word, we immediately knew what we were going to do. Yes, that's right. We knew each other so well. We could understand what was on each other's minds without saying one word. We went back into my room to hide him under my cot. I believed that our school class teacher was an incarnation of the devil and would throw a curse on us if he saw Buddy on the trip.

That being said, we ended up taking Buddy on the school trip. Why? Because that's just who we are. We take risks in life. Also, we were terrified my mother would find him. He was tiny enough to fit in my pink picnic basket which we covered with a white cotton picnic cloth. We settled into the last seats of the school bus. I knew the look in Riya's eyes. This was going to be one hell of an adventure; we shared a wicked smile.

We reached our destination in a couple of hours. I leaned on Riya's shoulder the whole time and felt like I was in the safest place, ever. We settled down in the park, shortly after which rain started pouring down on us. Buddy was with us the entire time–sleeping in the basket. He wouldn't make one sound as long as we were with him.

Both of us went to a secluded spot to look at Buddy. I gently lifted the white cloth off of the corner of the basket to feed him something. Riya brought canine biscuits because of the generous and thoughtful person that she is.

It was just a moment later that I realized I was alone with Buddy. He started whining as the water poured all over him. I panicked and felt my breath quickening. I was all alone in a new city with a whining dog. There was a building behind me, and I knew Riya would be using the washroom there. The building looked like it was built back in the 1800s. But I just couldn't leave her there. Without waiting for another second, I carried Buddy in my arms and dashed into the building. The building looked fragile and could be demolished at any time.

The plan was to get Riya and me outside and with the other

children as soon as possible. I noticed a gigantic door towards the end of a long corridor. I started running towards it—dripping wet, with Buddy running by my side.

I reached the door in what seemed like one whole day. I pushed open the door using my entire body weight, praying it was the washroom. Voila! It was! It was the dirtiest washroom I had seen in my entire life, from cobwebs to bugs, it seemed like no one had been there for a century now.

As I began to leave the washroom and started to wonder about where the hell Riya was, I felt a lightweight on my right shoulder. I swear, I did not want to know who that was.

I kept walking forward and by this time, 90% of the wetness on my body was just sweat pouring out of me from fear. I heard footsteps behind me and that's when I remembered my mother.

I swore under my breath and asked my mother for forgiveness. This was it, the last few moments of my life. I realized where I was and knew the main entrance was towards my left. I ran for my life, with Buddy running with me, with a confused look on his face. Yes, Buddy had expressions.

I jolted outside the entrance of the building to be welcomed by the sweet earthy smell of mother earth. The sun was out, and the rain had stopped by now. Buddy was by my side the whole time and I was almost in tears. It wasn't the best feeling in the world to be chased down by a ghost, but also, I felt the adventurer in me soothed.

'Finally!' I sighed.

As I turned around for the first time in what felt like a few years, I saw Riya's red face huffing and puffing. She looked like she wanted to kill me. For a second, I wasn't sure if she was the ghost I was escaping from.

But upon seeing her, I couldn't help myself but bolt out to throw myself on her. I felt my soul re-entering my body. For the first time,

I was laughing and crying at the same time.

Riya was all I needed. She was my entire world and the thought of losing her was the scariest thing I had ever thought of. I didn't have the guts to ask her if she was the one following me all that time, just because if the answer was no, I would stop going on adventures. I melted inside her arms just like her homemade chocolates would melt in my mouth.

But, at the end of the story, we were safe, all three of us. Buddy was meant to come with us on this trip- to stay by our side. We returned home on the bus, still wet. We were too exhausted to make attempts to hide Buddy from the teacher and students. I had already faced hell.

The teacher and children were surprisingly not mad at us for bringing him. It went well. We reached my doorstep to find my mother chatting with another strange-looking lady. They turned together toward us and flashed big smiles. Their smiles did not make me very happy. Something seemed off. The strange lady bent towards Buddy to touch him as he snapped at her.

'Buddy is her dog,' Mom said as she tilted her head sympathetically towards me.

I wanted to say a million things right then, but nothing seemed to leave my lips. Riya burst into tears, and I guarded Buddy to prevent her from reaching him.

'I lost my dog years ago,' she said as she showed me a picture of a tiny dog that looked like Buddy.

'NO!' I screamed.

I was not ready to see anyone claim Buddy to be their dog. At the same time, Riya turned towards me, apologetically nodding her head as a yes. I immediately knew what she meant. If we loved him, his owner loved him, too.

It was at that exact moment I realized; I wanted nothing more than for him to be happy. The lady scanned the identity chip in Buddy's locket and proved to me of him being her dog.

'Are you ok?' she asked, noticing my quietness in the past few days.

I looked up as Riya looked at me with concern. I looked around to realize I was in my math class. It was a horrid dream. 'Totally perfect!' I lied.

Riya and I didn't speak anymore. It was one year since we had a fight after which she ended our friendship.

We shared the kind of love you only see in movies. I wasn't sure which part of my life was a dream and which was reality, anymore. There seemed to be a very fine line dividing both of them and I couldn't decide which was scarier, this dream or my existence.

As buddy lay on my lap, at home, all I wished, for now, was to dream of the connection we had, again—I wanted to feel her hug just one more time, even if only in my dreams.

2

Love's Lost Journey

Shay P. Kris

Five years ago, August 2016

"Clickety-clack" "Clickety-clack"

'The next train arriving at 3:38 on platform 5, is a slow 12-car local for Kalyan…,' said the announcement.

The train announcements continued, around the corner, there was a bunch of commuters waiting to get their snacks from the hawker while two aunties gossiped behind me. Amidst this chaos, I hoped to see her smiling face on one of the arriving trains as we had plans to meet each other here today.

As time flew, I was anxious about whether she would show up. I sat there at the station with my backpack beside me and a single red rose on my lap, waiting...

Six months earlier, February 2016

I was late again, as usual. I rushed out with breakfast in hand, hoping I could still catch my train which would now be a near-impossible feat. Having gotten on my old and doddering Honda Activa, I peeled out of my society early morning. After two roundabouts and one traffic signal, I reached the station parking and hopped off the scooter.

Huffing and puffing, I reached the platform just in time to see the train exiting the station. Now that I had time to catch my breath and drink some water, I pulled out my water bottle. My local train app showed the next train will be ten minutes later. With my headphones playing The Chainsmokers' "*Call You Mine*" I sat on a bench. I glanced up and was entranced to see the most beautiful girl wearing a black T-shirt and jeans, she stood across the track. She had delicate angelic features and big eyes. She stared intently at her phone while I stood there admiring her. I was riveted by her when my train arrived at the station and blocked my view. Dismayed, I got up and boarded the train, thinking I might not see her again.

I was engrossed in my phone, playing a video game when the train jolted, and a knee brushed against mine. I looked up to apologize and stared straight into the warmest hazel eyes I had ever seen. I was speechless. She apologized and went back to her phone. During the journey, I kept stealing glances at her, but she never once looked up from her phone. Soon, my station arrived, and I had to get to work.

The next day, I skipped my usual train for a chance to see her again. I didn't see her anywhere on the platform. I boarded the next train and sat down. As the train was leaving, I heard a 'clank' from the door. I looked up and saw her get on the train. I kept debating with myself on whether I should go and say 'Hi' to her. Finally, I decided to go for it and sat opposite her.

'Hi, I am Akarsha,' I introduced myself.

'Oh! Hi, I'm Vaani,' she said in a husky tone.

'Where are you heading?' I asked.

'College. What about you?' she asked.

'Work. (*I looked up*) Ah! My station has come. It was nice seeing you. Bye!' I waved goodbye.

I cursed under my breath for not having more time with her. For the rest of the day, I wore a smile. Some of my co-workers even commented on me having a bounce in my step.

With each upcoming day, we got to know each other a little better, exchanged phone numbers, and started texting non-stop. We chatted about almost everything: music, college, work, friends, and so on. Every day, we would meet on the platform and travel together. She lived close to my home, so I started picking her up every day and we'd go to the station together. We visited each other, spent weekends hanging out, and went out to the movies. As time passed my feelings deepened.

On the way back home one day, 'Akarsha, let's have another sleepover this weekend, my parents will be out-of-town anyways. They are okay with me staying with your family,' she said as she was riding a pillion with me.

'I will have to check with Mom,' I replied, surprised at the revelation. 'Oh! Your mom already knows. (*I paused*) Okay, then, what do you want to do this weekend? My internship ends on Friday,' I asked.

'Let's watch some classic horror films, have popcorn, and chill,' she said.

'But you hate horror films,' I reminded her.

'Yes, but you keep talking so much about them, I want to see what's all the fuss about. Don't you dare pick a scary film!' she said.

'Then what's a point of a horror film,' I asked with a laugh.

'I don't know, but no gory movies,' she replied.

'Fine, no gory but at least it should be scary. Please!' I insisted.

'Okay, if I don't like it, then we will stop the movie. Deal?' she said.

'Deal!' I agreed.

By the time we made the deal, we reached her society. She got off and waved goodbye. Smiling, I drove home, stopping at a local grocery store to pick up some snacks for our sleepover. I got home and spent some time with Mom and Dad. I was super jazzed since it was my last two days as an intern, and after 2 weeks college would start again. Work was hectic for the next two days and in addition to my regular duties, all interns had to go through the leaving process with HR, which was a tedious affair. I barely got to see or chat with Vaani for those two days. On Friday evening, I was finally free. My six-month internship had come to an end. It was a grueling yet fulfilling experience, but the travel would not have been half as rewarding if I had not met Vaani.

I left early on Friday, so I texted Vaani.

'Hey! I just left work. Are you done?' I asked.

'Hi! No, I am still in class. It finishes in some time,' she said.

'Should I come to the college gates?' I asked her.

'Sure, I will wait,' she said.

Since her college was nearby, I decided to walk over there and meet her. I popped in my headphones, selected my playlist, and started walking. Walking always helped me clear my thoughts but that was highly unlikely today on account of my footwear. The only part of my internship I disliked was the fact I had to wear heels, not pencil heels or platforms but Mary Jane's. They are truly not made for walking. Unfortunately, I didn't have another pair to change into.

After a while and a few blisters, I reached her college. She stood waiting for me.

'Hey, you are my lucky charm!' she exclaimed.

'Why? What happened?' I asked with curiosity.

'As I received your last text, the professor was called on for an important meeting, so he dismissed the class early,' she replied with a bright smile.

'So, you have been waiting here since? Why didn't you call me? I would have come by cab then,' I said.

'Yea, maybe I should have called. I was glad that we were dismissed early and that I went to the canteen with my friends to get some chips. I got you your favorite ones,' she said.

'It's okay! Let's get going otherwise we will miss our train,' I said as I tried to stop a cab. We reached the station 15 mins later. She chatted incessantly throughout the journey back home.

'I want to get some stuff from home,' she said as I was driving my scooter out of the parking area.

'Okay,' I said.

As we reached her place, she invited me in. I sat on the sofa in her living room, waiting for her to collect her stuff and then we headed home.

'Akarsha, Vaani I have kept some pakoras on the dining table,' Mom said.

'Thanks, Auntie,' Vaani said.

'You are welcome, dear. (*She paused*) And by the way, we are going out tonight for a party and will be home late,' Mom said to me.

'What party?' unaware I asked.

'Uff! Some business party, one of those things your father drags me to every couple of months,' Mom replied and left.

'Cool, it looks like we have the house all to ourselves. So, what do you want to do first?' I asked Vaani.

'Let's finish these pakoras and then go and play some video games,' she said.

'Grab the plate; we'll eat in my room,' I said and grabbed my laptop.

We headed to my bedroom, opened our laptops, and started playing an online multiplayer game we were obsessed with. Pretty soon, all the pakoras were gone, and we were deciding on dinner.

'How about pizza?' she asked.

'Yes, let's go Domino's,' I said, and we preceded.

We locked up the apartment and went. On the way back, Vaani wanted to play Truth or Dare. I was skeptical but agreed to it.

'Got a coin? We'll flip for it. Your call,' she said.

I handed her a coin and called "heads" and I lost.

'Truth or Dare,' she asked smiling.

'Truth!' I replied with a Cheshire cat smile. What she didn't know was that when I play truth or dare, I never choose to dare, ever.

'Have you ever had a crush on someone?' she asked.

I cleared my throat. 'Wow, a tough question right at the start, huh? No, I don't have a crush on anyone. Your turn: Truth or dare?'

I lied.

Every time it was her turn, she chose to dare. By now I was running out of options.

'Take one dare at least. Come on!' she insisted.

'Ok, fine. Dare!' I spoke.

'I dare you to...' my heart was pounding. I have never taken a dare before, and I didn't want to do anything embarrassing.

'...kiss me,' she said.

'What?!' I didn't hear her the first time.

'I said, I dare you to kiss me!' she replied.

'Are you sure?' I asked sceptically.

'Yes, I am surprised you haven't till now, do it fast,' she said, 'I know that you have liked me for some time, and I like you too.'

As soon as she said that, I pulled her into my arms and kissed her.

Little did I know my first kiss would be this magical. I felt like floating in the air. Her soft lips were like velvet. She kissed me back. After what felt like an eternity, we broke apart for air and smiled at each other. Soon my parents came home.

For the rest of the weekend, we stole glances at each other and smiled fondly at the memory of our kiss. On Sunday evening, I asked her out on a date. We agreed to meet at the train station platform the following Friday.

***

Present day, 27th December 2021

No matter which country I live in, I am always late for the train. It's been a year since I moved to Australia. I had to catch the early morning light rail at Randwick bound for Town Hall. Which is usually a 15-minute walk to the station, was a 7-minute run for me today.

Luckily, I caught the train and reached before my boss got in.

'You could have woken me up, you know!' I told my girlfriend as I sat down at my desk. Leslie was our boss's PA. We started dating eight months ago.

'I did, and so did the alarm! It's not my fault if you can't hear either of us,' she quipped.

I stared at her, unamused as the ancient monitor in front of me groaned to life. The entire computer system was old and would shut down suddenly and unexpectedly.

'What time are you coming over tonight? I am making stew and salad,' I asked Leslie.

'I'll be leaving with you,' she replied.

The rest of the day droned on, as usual. I was bogged down with useless statistical data. I spent most of my day correcting my predecessor's work. By evening, it was time to leave. We left for the station together and caught the train.

We were chatting on the platform when suddenly I saw a familiar face in the crowd. Someone I haven't seen in five years.

It was Vaani! She no longer looked the same. She looked worn out and tired as she stood there chastising the toddler beside her. Suddenly, twin pairs of hazel eyes looked at me as I clutched Leslie's hand and fell back into a kaleidoscope of memories.

3

Love's Brief Repast

Shay P. Kris

A week ago,

'Hey babe, are you okay?' worried, my girlfriend asked.

Unable to answer, I just looked at her.

'Leslie, I...I... am okay,' I replied as I looked back across the platform and couldn't see those hazel eyes anywhere.

'Sweety, you don't look okay. Let's go home and I will make you a hot cup of tea,' she replied as she coaxed me onto the train.

***

January 2022

Leslie and I rang in the New Year with her family. I finally got to meet her parents Matt and Jody, who were pretty welcoming, and her siblings, John and Paul. John was home for the holidays, and it was Paul's last New Year as he was moving to London. All in all, it was a good weekend trip. John and Paul's incessant ribbing and jokes kept us thoroughly entertained during our trip to Melbourne. Jody's cooking will keep me in the gym for months to come just to work off all the holiday weight I gained. Leslie was truly in her element at her parent's farm. I got to ride horses, milk a cow for the first time, and spend some quality time with my girl.

But during the quiet weekend, my mind wandered towards Vaani. Seeing those hazel eyes again was a surprise I was not expecting and the child with her was even more so. So many questions are running through my head right now. I want answers to these questions, but I don't know if our paths will cross again.

Today has been a hectic day from start to finish. Work was good today, finally having finished tackling my predecessor's incorrect work, I joined my boss and a few of our sales team members for the sales pitch for new clients. After onboarding 4 clients today, I was bone tired and just wanted to soak in a warm bath. I said goodbye to Leslie and went home. I got on my usual train when I got a message from Leslie. She told me not to wait for her as she will be late and will have dinner outside before coming over. Smiling, I messaged her back a smiley and party emoji. Since she disliked the smell of raw fish, I couldn't eat sushi around her. I decided to stop by the sushi place near my apartment on my way back. I had another 15 mins to go before I reached my stop when I felt I was being watched, and I looked up from my phone.

Déjà vu!

I was sitting across from Vaani again. She was alone this time. I just stared at her for what seemed like a few minutes.

'Hi, (*I paused*) It's been a long time,' I said, trying to break the awkward silence.

'Hi, Akarsha,' She replied in a polite, but weak tone.

'How have you been? When did you come to Australia?' I asked trying to be inquisitive yet lacking the courage to ask her the question that I wanted to ask.

'I have been good; life is not what I expected. I moved here after my marriage,' She replied.

'Wow! When did you get married?' I asked and 'Akarsha, I am sorry!' We both spoke at the same time. Before either of us could reply, the train doors dinged for my stop.

'Hey, there's a cute little café down the street outside the station. Want to get a cup of coffee?' I asked her, as I was getting ready to deboard the train.

'No, not today. Some other time, perhaps,' she replied as she got up and moved to a seat closer to the door.

I waved her goodbye and walked home.

I was seeing Vaani after all these years has opened up old wounds. Part of me wants to know why she left me behind and, the other doesn't want an answer. Since the first time I saw her on the platform last week, I haven't been feeling myself. I have just been going through the motions. I feel restless and weary at the same time. Up until now, I have been using work as an escape, but over the past week, it was anything but an escape. I keep replaying the scene at the station over and over again in mind, wondering what the different outcomes might have been. What if Leslie hadn't been there, would I have walked up to Vaani and spoken to her?

Oh god! Leslie. What do I tell her? I know I don't have any romantic feelings for Vaani anymore and I love Leslie but with Vaani back in my life, where does it go from here?

Immersed in my thoughts, I realized I hadn't picked up any dinner. I dropped my bag and keys on the dining table and sent a text message to Leslie.

"Where are you?"

"Just left the office," she replied.

"Can you get some dinner?"

"Burger n fries?" she asked.

"Sure. See you."

Since Leslie was picking up dinner, I went to freshen up and then set the table with cutlery and plates.

'Hey honey, I'm home,' Leslie hollered from the door as I was collecting the glasses and water.

'Why didn't you pick up sushi for yourself today? You usually do when you send me the party emoji,' she asked as she unwrapped the food and plated it.

'It just slipped out of my mind. I didn't realize it till I got to the door,' I replied wanting to avoid the "Vaani" conversation.

We spent the next half hour at the dinner table talking about our day. One of our co-workers recently got a really bad haircut and somehow, we were discussing it.

'Poor May! I hope she gave her stylist a firing. It truly is a bad haircut,' I said as I started doing the dishes.

'I know, I wonder what style she picked at the beginning of the session,' she replied as she was drying the washed dishes and arranging them.

'Whatever it was, it surely wasn't the one she has now,' I smiled at her triumphantly as I finished washing all the dishes.

'I'll grab the wine; you pick a movie,' she said picking out the wine glasses.

I found the TV remote among all the fluffy pillows and sat on my plush second-hand sofa. Scrolling through Amazon Prime, I was unsure what to watch.

'Kash, which wine would you like to have?' Leslie called out from the kitchen.

'White!' I replied grudgingly, I always hated that nickname, but it was not the worst I was called.

'I hate it when you call me Kash,' I told her as she handed me my glass and sat down next to me.

'I know,' she replied, wiggling her eyebrows. Whenever she is in a good mood and wants her way, she does this. I smiled at her and pulled her close, kissed her on the forehead, and then turned to the TV. I picked some mind-numbing comedy shows just to pass the time.

After drinking the last sip of my wine, I shut off the TV abruptly.

'Hey, I was watching that,' Leslie sort of jostled herself awake from her light nap.

'Les, we need to talk,' I replied, steeling myself for what may happen next.

'Sure honey. What about?' she asked curiously.

'Remember last week at the station, I looked like I had seen a ghost?' I asked cautiously.

'Yeah?' She sat up, clearly hearing the tone of my voice.

'Well in a way I had,' I continued the tell her everything about Vaani. About how we met, our relationship, and how she left me standing at the station. She listened attentively as I told her about tonight as well and explained to her why I missed picking up dinner. After I was done, I turned the conversation into a Q&A session and answered all her doubts including whether I still had feelings for Vaani. Afterward, we cleaned up and went to bed.

The next day, we both got to work on time after breakfast. During the day, I headed out with the sales team to meet a client. After we met with the client, they introduced us to their legal team for the contracts. As we entered the client's cabin, I saw Vaani sitting there looking surprised to see me. The client introduced my team to her and then we got down to the contracts. I was so starstruck that I didn't correct Mack when he introduced me.

After the meeting, I invited Vaani out for lunch. We ended up in a tiny bistro near the business plaza. We caught up on a lot of things and by the end of lunch, we fell back into old patterns. We reminisced about college, street food, and festivals.

'Why didn't you show up all those years ago or call or text?' I asked Vaani as I walked her to her office.

'I couldn't show up that day. I am sorry I didn't message you. Sometimes, I wish I had met you that day, who knows where we would have been then?' She replied quietly as if trying to end the conversation there.

'I deserve to know why I was left standing on that platform with a rose,' I countered forcefully.

'I will tell you one day, but not today. Let's meet for coffee sometime soon. Give me your number, and I will text you the address,' she replied trying to ease the conversation with a smile.

28th January 2022

For the last two weeks, Vaani and I have been meeting at cafés and bistros near work and home. Nothing untoward. Just catching up and rebuilding our friendship. She confided in me about what happened five years back, her unhappy marriage, and her family troubles. Finally, after all these years, I got closure and was able to forgive her too. We decide that we were better off as friends, even if neither of us regretted our past.

Today, I received a text from Vaani. She wanted to meet at 1 pm near the coffee place around the corner from my office. I had an early lunch and went to meet her.

'Hey!' I beamed at Vaani.

'Hi! I was in the neighbourhood, so I texted you,' smiling, she replied. We hugged and went to a seat near the window.

'So how is your day going?' I asked her as I was browsing the menu.

'Just travelling around as usual. How about you?' She replied as she tried to catch the barista's attention.

'Same old, rotting behind a desk,' I smirked at her.

We replayed our order to the barista and continued talking about our respective weekends. She went on a trek with her friends. I spent mine bored to death while Leslie shopped non-stop at the mall. We had our food, and the barista cleared our plates. We were just sipping on our beverages when someone put their hand on my shoulder.

'Oh, hi! What are you doing here?' I asked, surprised, seeing Leslie standing behind me.

'I was just on my way back from running an errand for our boss. Aren't you going to introduce us?' Leslie replied smiling.

'Oh! I am sorry. Les...' I was immediately interrupted.

'Hi, my name is Vaani!' Vaani said.

4

Love's Enduring Vow

Shay P. Kris

May 2026

Beep…Beep…

'Ugh, we are late again!' I thought to myself as the alarm beeped at quarter past 7.

'Leslie, get up! We are late!' I said as I tried to jostle her awake.

'Come on, we are going to be late!' I continued as I stumbled around putting on my pants.

'What is going on about?' she asked groggily.

'I'll walk Taffy and you get the kids ready for daycare or else we'll be late for work. Get up!' I said as I was half dressed, trying to pull the covers off Leslie.

'Honey, it's Sunday! Go back to sleep,' she replied as she successfully won the covers battle.

'No, it's…Monday…oops. Sorry, my bad! Ever since the twins turned 2, I haven't been able to tell heads from tails,' I replied sheepishly as she stared at me unamused. I quickly changed back into my PJs and got back into bed with Leslie.

'I am sorry for waking you up like that on a Sunday. What can I do to make it up to you?' I asked.

'Well, we have a moment till the kids wake up, what do you say we…Goo…Goo...Baa…', just when Leslie was about to complete her thought, we heard the twins on the baby monitor.

'Looks like we are out of time,' I smiled as I jumped out of bed. Leslie smiled back knowing all too well that we won't get any time together till the kids were asleep at night.

A little orange ball of fluff rushed into our bedroom as soon as I opened the door. Our little Taffy got on the bed with Leslie's help and set about to give her some morning licks.

'Taffy…stop!' I heard Leslie admonish our corgi as I entered the twins' nursery next door.

'Good morning Mavey! Good morning, Joni!' Both girls gave me dazzling smiles.

I lifted Joni to check on her nappy when Leslie entered.

'Hi, Mavey baby! Come to Mama,' just as Leslie picked up Mavis, the doorbell rang.

'I'll get it,' I rushed to the door as fast as I could with a 2-year-old in my arms, all the while trying not to trip over Taffy. I opened the front door only to find a woman and a police officer at our doorstep.

'Good morning! Is there something I can help you with?' I asked them.

***

Four years ago, January 2022

I ran after Leslie as she exited the coffee shop.

'Wait, Leslie, let me explain,' I said as she stopped at the garden in front of our office.

'What is there to explain? You are still in love with your ex?' She replied in a huff.

'No, I am not. I love you. I just want to talk to her…' I spoke.

'Talk about what? Huh! (*She paused*) About why she left or about how the two of you can get back together?' she asked.

'Leslie, please try to understand that meeting her over the past couple of weeks was about trying to repair our friendship,' I pleaded with her.

'Past couple of weeks? Sneaking around with your ex, for the past couple of weeks?' The tenor of her voice indicated to me that she was angry.

'There was no sneaking around. I am not cheating on you or any such thing, okay? I am just a friend trying to help her through some bad times. Honest!' I replied, trying to de-escalate the situation.

'Then why have you been so on edge these past couple of weeks?' she asked.

'I have not been on edge. I have just…I don't know what I am doing. Please just give me some time. Let's talk tonight at home, ok?' I tried to calm her down.

'No, let's talk now,' she said.

'Okay!' Dismayed, I took a seat on the nearby garden bench. I told her the whole story- everything for what seemed like forever. At the end of it, Leslie told me that we needed a time-out. She insisted that I have to decide on what I wanted and walked away.

When I got back to the office ten minutes later, she was talking to our boss. A few minutes later she came out and sat at her desk, I went over to her.

'Leslie…I' I wanted to apologize, but she interrupted.

'I am taking a few weeks off; I have two weeks' leave pending from last year and I will lose them soon. I am going to my parent's place.

Please don't contact me till you have figured out what you want and where I fit in it,' with that she left, leaving me heartbroken and unsure about what to do next. I was devastated that she just left.

Days flew by. The one thing I was sure of was that I wanted Leslie in my life. I loved her but I had this nagging feeling that without knowing the truth, I may never be able to move on. I need to move on, Leslie needs me to move on.

So, on Thursday, I decide to meet Vaani one more time.

Me: Meet me for dinner today.

Vaani: Ok, I need to rearrange a few things. When? Where?

Me: 7:30, Giovanni's- next to your office.

Vaani: Ok, bye.

Post lunch, work was great but slow. Our boss came into the bullpen at around four to announce that we had an exemplary last quarter and that we were getting a bonus. A cacophony of cheers broke out after the announcement. All my colleagues were planning a dinner and pub crawl this weekend. I was happy that all our hard work paid off, I picked up my phone and almost dialled Leslie's number. I missed her. I resumed work, hoping after today I would have my answers and get Leslie back.

Since it's about a half-hour walk to Giovanni's, I left the office at around 7. I wanted to get there a couple of minutes early so I could order their fabulous molten garlic bread. I reached the restaurant just in time to place my order, I swear they just fly off the shelves on most days.

Vaani arrived a few minutes after I did, and we got a table near a window.

'So how was your day?' she asked as she settled herself across from me.

'It was good, got a bonus,' I replied with a wry smile as I looked over the drinks list.

'Oh! Congratulations. How is Leslie?' she asked.

'She is good. She has gone to visit her parents. I will go up there in a few days,' I said not wanting her to know about our break, it was true that I will be going there, just not sure when.

'Okay. I know what you want to talk about, and I am ready to tell you why I didn't meet you at the station that day,' Vaani gathered herself and said calmly.

Vaani spoke for what seemed like an hour, but the gist of the whole conversation was that she and her family were forced to move to another state because her dad got a new job and, in the move, she lost her phone and my number along with it. After this revelation, we quietly ate dinner and made small talk. After dinner, we split the check and parted ways outside the restaurant.

'Bye Vaani, call me when you want to catch up again,' I waved to her with a bright smile.

'Yeah, sure. I will let you know,' she replied with what seemed a sad smile. Before I could ask her about that, she walked away.

The whole way home, I was thinking about what Vaani said and wondered if all these years I had built it up in my head that she didn't want to be with me or something even worse. But her actual reason, however improbable seemed possible and hopefully true.

It's been weeks since I heard from Vaani, so I texted her. No reply yet. On a happier note, Leslie was back in the office. She wasn't giving me a cold shoulder, but we still haven't spoken to each other yet. God! I missed her smile. I missed everything about her- her breakfast, her insistence on holding hands on the train, our "Yes…No" fights.

It's all most our first anniversary and I knew what I wanted to get her. I have known for some time. So, I took a half day off work to prepare. I went down to the fashion district to visit a particular jewelry store to pick up her gift. I called ahead to look for something special for her.

I called her parents to check if she was spending our anniversary with them, and they were kind enough to let me in on her travel plans. So, I booked myself on an earlier train.

On our anniversary eve, I got to her parent's place half an hour before she did and put up the decorations with their help.

The clock went on and with each passing minute, I was equally nervous and excited.

'Hey Mom, I am home… Akarsha, what are you…oh my God!' As soon as she came through the front door, I got down on my knee with her gift- a teardrop-shaped diamond ring set in white gold.

'You mean more to me than breathing. I want to prove that to you for the rest of our lives. Will you marry me, Leslie?' Her parents cheered behind me.

'No!' She replied with a mischievous smile.

'Yes!' I laughed as I got to my feet and slid the ring on her finger.

No… Yes… No… I didn't give her another chance to say 'No' to me as I took her in a sweeping kiss, her parents and her brothers whistled, cheered, and congratulated us.

***

Present day, May 2026

'Are you Mrs. Tuffin-Singh? I am Aimee Marshall from Child Protection Services,' said the unknown lady at the door.

'Yes, I am. How can I help you?' I asked.

'Did you know a Mrs. Vaani Mehrotra?' Hearing Vaani's name again was like being hit by a freight train.

'Yes, I did. Is she ok?' I asked with a dry face.

'No, ma'am. She died about four years back and according to her will she named you her daughter's guardian,' she said and a little one came forth.

'I need to sit down, please come in,' I was shocked. I let the CPS officer and Vaani's daughter into the house.

'Honey, who was at the do…' Leslie walked into the living room with Joni. I introduced Leslie to Aimee and brought her up to speed. We settled the twins in their playpen and went back to talk to Aimee. She told us there was a misplacement of Vaani's will and because of that, her daughter was in foster care till now. The whole time Aimee was talking, all I could do was look at Vaani's daughter. She had her eyes. She had no living relatives, and her father was not in the picture. She stood there near the sofa in a pale-yellow frock clutching onto a raggedy old teddy bear which was almost grey now.

Aimee and Leslie spoke for about half an hour about the foster and adoption process. Just before Aimee left, she told us the little girl doesn't speak- she is not mute, she just doesn't speak. With that, she was off and would visit again in a week to check on us.

Leslie spoke to the little girl and welcomed her into our home. She introduced us, our girls, and our dog. The little girl seemed curious about the dog but was a little timid about petting him. We went about our day accommodating the little girl into our plans and soon into our life. By nighttime we were exhausted with kids. We set up the guest room for the girl and went out clothes shopping for her. We picked up stuff that seemed to pique her interest as she still hadn't said a word.

A few days later, around midnight, I got out of bed and went to the kitchen. On the way back, I looked in on the little girl. Her teddy bear was on the ground. I went to pick it up and saw that one of its buttons was missing.

I quietly took the teddy bear to the living room and got the sewing kit. I set about fixing the teddy's eye when I felt the crinkle of paper from inside the teddy. I carefully removed the stitches and removed the paper from inside it.

It was a letter from Vaani!

Dear Akarsha,

Somehow, I knew this little, tiny teddy would fall into your hands someday, in case I succumb to stage 4 pancreatic cancer, so this seemed to be the perfect place to hide this letter. I always wanted to tell you a few other things that I could not do at the Giovanni's. My parents figured out that, I am a lesbian, and hence wanted me to get married to the guy of their choice. It did not turn out well and I kept looking for you. Now that is my daughter, Avyukta. A few months down the line after her birth, my husband left both of us, to shack up with his girlfriend. I knew I would die, just wasn't courageous enough to say that. I seek no forgiveness, but I trust no one on this planet to take care of my daughter, but you. You promised me you would always be there for me. Now I need you to be there for my baby girl. For my Avyukta!

Love you, always.

Forever yours,

Vaani

5

Little Infinities

Vanshika Gupta

It was 20th December 2011, the most exciting day for the students of the 9th standard as we were about to have the most awaited class photograph of the session. I was in the school choir and rushed towards the auditorium where all the sections were asked to gather in line for the photograph. Call it the perks of being in the school choir on the usual days, as I relished my zero period, singing and rehearsing the prayers for the next day while other students in my class had to brace themselves up for the frightening current affairs quiz, unlike today.

As I was just about to open the door of the auditorium, one of my friends shouted my name from behind and I was standing there all confused because I didn't expect to see her outside at this hour.

'You just have to listen to this, Vaarya!', panting and running towards me, Ria was all worked up. I calmed her down and asked her what was this about and why was she not inside with the rest of our classmates.

'You won't believe it, but this news is certainly the news of the month! So, today before the morning assembly, Kartik told Jay that he likes somebody from our section, and guess what, her name ends with "A"!' Ria said with a wicked smile on her face.

I acted like it was not such a big deal, and went inside the auditorium with her as she, like the rest of the students, could not afford to miss out on the only group photograph of our class while for me, it barely mattered. The hall was full of the 9th class students along with their class teachers and the school Principal. There I spotted Kartik from section A, and all I wanted to do was punch him in the face for not telling me about his 'new crush' earlier.

Yes. A punch right in the face. Kartik was not my best friend but my favorite friend and how could he not be? We had been in the same section for the past 8 years and he was the only boy from our class whose name I never missed writing on the "Blackstar section" on the blackboard while monitoring the class; he was extremely annoying and talkative. We didn't have normal conversations. All we did was hit each other. While he used to pull my ponytail now and then, I used to run after him with the blackboard duster in my hands. But despite it all, we were the coolest buddies in our class. Sadly, our sections got reshuffled and he went to section A, while I remained in B.

After the photographs were taken, our class teachers instructed us to go to our respective sections in a line. The new Principal had these strict rules and made sure that nobody dared to disobey any and so walking in a queue became the new normal for our school. As soon as we reached the corridor, I stepped outside the line and searched for Kartik. He came from the washroom and ignored me like I wasn't even there. He was getting on my nerves. I called him and asked him why he was being so rude that he didn't even bother to look at me, forgetting to tell me about his new crush.

'I'm so sorry Vaarya, I didn't see you, and to be honest, I'm not in my right mind at the moment,' he sounded low. I asked him if everything was alright. He said that he was fine but was bothered about some stupid rumour about him, that everyone had now started teasing him.

'I know about it, Kartik. I wanted to know this from you and not from others,' I replied.

He asked me to believe in him and that when he finds somebody, I will be the first one to know about it. I was assured and happy. After our regular fist bump, both of us went to our respective classes.

While I was trying to concentrate on the Science class, my other friends along with Ria were guessing the name of Kartik's new crush and started listing down the name of every single girl from our class, whose name ended with "A". I didn't bother much because I knew that all these rumours were false. I told my friends to stop thinking about it and rather concentrate on the class as there were only 2-3 months to go before the final exams. They ignored my words and just continued with the list. I started paying more attention to the teacher rather than these fools. It was all going well until I heard Ria saying that my name on the list was out of the question and thus, chopped off my name from the list. I don't know why and neither did I expect or want Kartik to like me but, I felt dejected.

With all the hush and rush, school was over and for the first time, I left school without him. He always accompanied me on the school bus and then walked towards his home as his home was within walking distance from our school. I asked Jay about him, and he told me that he was off the whole day. I knew it must have been about the false rumours and told Jay the same.

He asserted that these were no false rumours and that he liked the mysterious "A" girl. Jay was our common friend and was now afraid that Kartik would be mad at him for creating a ruckus out of this confession. I was clueless and speechless. With the last horn, my mind gained consciousness and I went inside the bus.

Ever since I heard about this rumour, my heart has not at rest. The news of his liking had me all anxious and worried. I found myself, badly wishing for these rumours to be untrue.

Well, the next day when I reached school, my class corridor was absurdly quiet as if all the students were absent. I went ahead and boom! Ria scared the hell out of me by pushing me from behind the otherwise lonely corridor. I was in no mood for all this and asked her to stay away. Overexcited as she always was, she dragged me towards the other end of the corridor where all the students of our class had gathered. I had no idea about what was going on and then, appeared that dumb guy with a red rose in his hand. My mind went numb in the increasing chaos and I couldn't fathom anything. The only thing that I am sure of hearing was Kartik saying,

'I like you a lot Vaarya and I want you to be my girlfriend.'

With a blank mind, I kept staring at Kartik. My friends on one side encouraged me to say yes along with his friends. I had so many questions for him, but I couldn't utter a word in front of him, except an "Okay!"

And hence, our relationship started with an awkward "Okay!"

I had always been the shy girl for the entire school, except for Kartik. He knew the real me. I soon realized that whatever I was feeling after the rumours was nothing else but the fear of losing my favorite friend, and in no time, we both fell for each other. We had our cute gestures and the only thing that gave me the chills down my spine except for a cup of tea was our eye contact. Whether it was the shine of his spectacles or his side dimple, just eye contact with him made my entire day. It was the little things for us. From risking my life on disguising his landline call from Ria to getting nervous with the first hug after our relationship to secretly meeting in the school garden, we lived all of it, from the fear of getting caught by the teachers to the fun of escaping through the class.

I remember around that time, the then heartthrob Ranbir Kapoor's 'Rockstar' had been released, and though it was a big musical hit, one track that had touched my soul straight was "*Tum*

Ho, (You are...)" in the magical voice of Mohit Chauhan. The moment I heard it, I decided to dedicate this song to Kartik in our school fest and, I did it and that's how it became–Vaarya and Kartik's song. My friends used to say that after his confession I was on cloud nine and I couldn't deny any of it. I was dating my favorite friend. I found no reason to be normal.

We all got busy with exams and soon after, we had our summer vacations. We didn't talk much during the vacations because we didn't have our phones and the landline call was a terrible idea. At that time, I wrote letters to Kartik, whenever I missed him, or whether I had to tell him about the new movie character I had fantasized about. I thought of giving him these letters after the vacations were over but then, kept them to myself as I feel that some things are too good to be shared. After the vacation when we saw each other, Kartik hugged me tightly in his arms and said that he missed me a lot. I was dying to see him too. Only if his grandparents' house was not that far from our city, we would have met each other.

Days after days, I felt that something was fading from our relationship. Now we didn't talk like we used to, and I knew that it happens, maybe we needed more time with each other. The most important thing in a relationship is friendship and I realized that now, we were no longer those buddies. Our conversations had dropped to just eye contact. But relationships don't work only on eye contact. Whenever I met him, I felt strong energy in his eyes that told me that he loved me, and I was assured. But as time passed, we found it difficult to even have simple conversations. One of our classmates mocked us saying that we both should better talk with eyes only, words won't work in our case. While Kartik was disturbed by his comment, I couldn't agree more with him.

One day after gathering a lot of courage, Kartik came to me and suggested that we should rather break up. '*We don't talk much, and this has spoiled our friendship too, we should just remain as friends,*' Kartik said with a lot of hesitation, but I could feel the conviction in his voice.

I agreed with him and thought that doing this would at least save our friendship as I couldn't afford to lose him completely.

Just like it began with an okay, it ended with just an okay.

Nothing was the same. We had grown mature, and we understood the fact that it's easier said than done when it comes to being friends after a breakup. I knew in my heart that he still loved me. They say that the truth is reflected in a person's eyes and his eyes spoke of this truth. I too loved him with all my heart, but being together was not the way for us.

We were now in 12th and the pressure for a non-medical student is something anyone would empathize with. We both were in the same stream but in different sections. Somewhere in the mid-session, I found out that Kartik was dating one of our juniors. I was so mad at him and felt like he betrayed me. With a heavy heart, I congratulated him through my Facebook account. I didn't expect a reply, but he did. "Thank you Vaarya, hope you are doing well!"

"*Well. You asshole!*" I thought to myself and didn't bother to reply. We barely talked in school and forgot about the social sites, I felt like blocking him from each one of them. The only thing that I was not able to decipher was my growing love for him and his changing love for me.

Is it possible that we can love twice? How do people fall out of love? What is love in its true sense? My mind was full of these questions to which nobody had a good answer.

10 years down, when I look back at the school going Vaarya with her understanding of love and betrayal, I feel like teleporting to that time when my younger self was full of bitterness towards love and questioned the credibility and idea of true love. Today, when I am well settled and happy with my solitude, I am taking the courage to write the last letter to my first love.

Dear Kartik,

I know it has been too long since I've written to you, but I want you to know that you did nothing wrong. I made you a criminal in my mind for a long time, but I understood with time, that when it comes to love, time doesn't matter. We loved each other truly in our time. Falling out of love cannot be contained but while you fell out of love with me, I fell out of faith in myself. Today I'm here, much stronger and wiser. Thank you for being my favorite friend once and for not betraying me for real.

Good wishes always.

Vaarya

Just like the other letters, Kartik won't receive this too and it's not really for him. It's for my peace. It's for me to know that sometimes people end up together and sometimes they don't, and if today we both are on our separate paths, it was our fate to be at our best, but on our own. He will always hold a piece of my heart, but the rest of my heart belongs to me and maybe at the right time, I'll find the right one to share it with. I've freed myself from all the bitterness that I had surrounded myself with, and with my arms wide open, I'm here for all that this life has in its store to bless me with.

Let us all believe in this magic of time. Let us give time some time, and I'm sure that it won't disappoint us.

6

The One

Surya Sai Prasanth Palaparthy

One evening, Secunderabad railway station.

A 60-year-old man was waiting on platform number 10 for the Rajdhani Express coming from Delhi. He was traveling to Bangalore for a special occasion. It was winter and a cold wave warning was given just a few days earlier. The old man could feel the freezing air on his fragile and old skin. Just a few steps away was a young couple waiting for the same train. Suddenly they start to quarrel about something. Realizing that they were at a train station, they became silent. The train which was supposed to come at half past 6 in the evening arrived 15 minutes before. The old man had only one small bag. As the train halted, he boarded and sat at his place. He always travelled in AC 2-tier as it was calmer than the 3-tier and a bit less expensive than the 1-tier. Through the window, he sees the young couple just standing silently and holding hands. The girl's eyes were teary while the boy tried to hold his tears back. They just stood silent, and not even looked at each other. Just then the station master waved a green flag as a signal that it was time to depart. Just then the boy hugged the girl and kissed her on the forehead, still trying to hold his tears. The train then started to move, and the boy unwillingly walked the girl to the train. They hugged for one last time and the girl boarded the train, still crying. The train paced up. With vain efforts in controlling tears, the boy cried.

The AC 2-tier compartment hardly had a few people. The girl walks slowly as if she lost everything and sits opposite the old man. After a few minutes, the old man in an attempt to console her, initiated a conversation.

'Is everything alright?' he asked.

The girl just nodded her head.

A few minutes passed by, and the girl stopped crying, and just stared out through the window into the darkness.

'My name is Ayrus,' said the old man.

'Keerthi,' said the girl in a broken voice without even turning her head.

Just then Ayrus started coughing badly and put a handkerchief against his mouth. Keerthi offered him some water and noticed that the old man was coughing blood. Ayrus took the water bottle, went near the wash basin, gargled some water, washed his face, and came back.

'Are you alright uncle?' Keerthi asked.

'Yes,' said Ayrus.

'Are you sure? I noticed you coughed some blood,' said Keerthi.

'It is just a medication side-effect,' said Ayrus.

'How are you feeling now?' Ayrus asked.

'Better,' (*Smiled*) said Keerthi.

'May I ask why you and the young man were crying?' Ayrus asked.

'I am going to Bangalore for a job, and he got a job here in

Hyderabad. We have never been far apart…' Keerthi breaks into tears.

'It felt as if I was seeing my past,' Ayrus said with a smile.

'A similar thing happened 35 years ago, at the same station as me and the love of my life, were coming back from Bangalore in this very train,' Ayrus continued.

'Love of your life, that's interesting. Where is she now?' asked Keerthi.

Ayrus opened his wallet and handed over a photo of Khushi.

"The love of my life," was written on the backside.

'She is very pretty,' said Keerthi.

'Thank you,' Ayrus blushed.

'Where is she now? How did you guys meet? Did you get married?' asked Keerthi.

Ayrus smiled, paused, and said 'The weather in Bangalore is very unusual and just. Even in winter, it feels like peak summer and in the very next second, it starts to rain. On one such rainy winter day…'

***

35 years ago, Bangalore

Young Ayrus, along with Khushi got down from a cab and rushed into a nearby mall as it was raining heavily. It was a bright sunny day when they planned, but by the time they reached it, it was already raining. It was their first date. Ayrus felt that the date would be ruined if it didn't stop raining.

'Let's go sit in the food court,' says Ayrus.

They ordered two coffees and a chocolate brownie. They start talking about various things like their past, lifestyle, etc. Just then Khushi takes her ring which she usually wears on her thumb and puts it on Ayrus's left-hand ring finger.

In the present, Keerthi noticed that the ring was still on his finger. Ayrus smiled and continued...

After putting the ring on, they noticed that the rain had stopped. They headed towards the terrace of the mall where there was a sitting area. They just sat and chatted, forgetting everything and everyone around them. After a while, Ayrus suggested going for a romantic walk to Cubbon Park, which was nearby.

As they walked at a slow pace, their hands intertwined for the first time, and both blushed a little. As they reached the park, it started to drizzle. But they continued to walk. Just talking and teasing each other, they reached about half the park and decided to stay there a little bit. They stood against a tree holding hands and looking into each other's eyes. Even though they did not say the words, they both knew exactly the other person's love language. They hugged. Ayrus and Khushi felt the time had stopped and felt safe in each other's company.

'What if my parents don't accept?' asked Khushi. Ayrus was from Hyderabad and Khushi was from Delhi.

'I will convince them,' Ayrus assured.

'But we are from completely different cultures,' Khushi said.

'Well, we will learn about each other's culture,' Ayrus said.

'What if your parents don't accept?' Khushi asked.

'Then we will convince them,' Ayrus assured.

'Whatever happens, we will be together forever, right?' he asked.

They looked into each other's eyes and kissed. After a few seconds, they realized they were in a park and people were watching. They walked out.

As days passed their bond became stronger. They were in Bangalore for training and two months later, they returned to their hometowns. (Ayrus to Hyderabad, Khushi to Delhi)

As soon as the train reached Hyderabad from Bangalore, they tried to hold back their tears and hugged. Days just passed by, and they missed each other. Days turned into months.

'Vexed with my job, and in the hope to get a new better job I resigned even after Khushi was reluctant,' Ayrus said as he held back his tears.

As days passed by things got worse in their lives and their relationship. He was unemployed and Khushi tried to balance her work life, her personal life, and her family.

Things between them became even worse. They, who once could not go an hour without talking just stopped talking for days together.

Amidst this phase, he got a job that he always wanted and went to Delhi to surprise Khushi. As soon as she saw him, Khushi ran towards her and hugged him. That's when they realized that their relationship was not dead after all and reconciled. Khushi took him to her home to meet her family. They were sweet people. They welcomed him and he spent a lot of time with them. He put forth his intentions to marry Khushi, which they happily accepted.

As they were going back to the airport…

Ayrus stopped, reaching for his water bottle and Keerthi looked at him anxiously; with why did you stop kind of look '…we had to take a different route as there was some strike happening. We were just minutes away from the airport, just an exit to the left from the highway and we would have entered the airport, I was holding Khushi's hand and was looking into her eyes, just then out of nowhere a big truck came at a full speed hit our car.'

Keerthi trembled a bit.

'The next thing I knew I was in a hospital with tubes all over my mouth and nose. The doctor rushed in, talking to me asking if I could see and hear. I saw my mother and my brother also rushing into the room crying,' said Ayrus.

'A few days later, all the tubes were removed, I asked the doctor how was Khushi, the girl who was with me in the car. The doctor replied that as the impact was on her side of the car, she died instantly,' Ayrus said wiping the tears rolling down his cheek.

Keerthi was shocked after hearing this.

'The last thing I remembered was her beautiful eyes and her smile. It has been 34 years since this happened. I neither loved anyone nor married because I was and still am in love with her, she was–the one,' Ayrus said seeing the photograph of Khushi and smiling while tears rolled down.

'Why are you going to Bangalore then?' asked Keerthi.

'It is our 35th anniversary tomorrow. Every year I spend our love anniversary in Bangalore, in Cubbon Park, under the tree where we had our first kiss,' Ayrus said.

Just then Keerthi gets a call, 'Why were you not picking up my call?' shouted Suresh from the other end.

'I was listening to a love story that happened 35 years back,' Keerthi replied smiling, and told Suresh the entire story.

Towards the end of the conversation, Suresh said, 'You have a surprise waiting in Bangalore.'

By the time Keerthi reached her berth, Ayrus was already asleep.

Keerthi also slept thinking about what the surprise might be.

The train reached KSR Bangalore station. Keerthi, who was already excited about the surprise jumps off the train as soon as the train stops. Keerthi calls Suresh and asks, 'Where is my surprise?'

'Right behind you madam!' a strange voice spoke.

Keerthi turns back and sees Suresh behind her. She was surprised and they hugged.

'What are you doing here? How did you get here?' Keerthi asked in a loud voice.

'I took an early flight...' said Suresh, 'to spend some time with you here in Bangalore.'

'But when I asked you to accompany me you told me that you cannot,' said Keerthi.

'After listening to the story of that old man Ayrus, I couldn't stop myself from coming to meet you,' he said.

Just then Ayrus got off the train, looked at them, and smiled.

7

Detour

Rohan P. Lapalikar

Siddharth while in his world and munching cookies walked through the stairs towards the 3rd floor of his school. Right there, he saw a boy from another class being bullied.

This part of the story is called–*The Fate.*

'Hey man, your nose looks fine. Would you like to have a red nose, huh?' Himesh asked in a fiend tone as he held Ishaan's collar.

'Hey, why don't we just throw him in a room full of girls and watch him shivering out of fear?' asked Anupam, Himesh's friend.

Moments before Himesh raised his hand to hit him in the face, Siddharth interrupted. 'Hey you swine, why don't you grow a pair of balls and come here and fight someone your size?' he asked in a valiant tone as he packed the cookie packet and kept it back in his pocket.

'Let's go Himesh, he might complain about us,' said Anupam, they left and ran back to their class.

Siddharth walked toward Ishaan and made sure he was okay.

'Hey! I am Siddharth, from 11th A,' he said.

With a confused look and gathering his fallen books, 'I am Ishaan. 11th C,' Ishaan said.

Siddharth bowed down to help him, and said, 'Here buddy, have a cookie.'

With a dicey look, Ishaan grabbed one and thanked him.

'It's super-tasty. Is it from some bakery?' Ishaan asked.

'Nope. My mum made them. Here, have some more,' Siddharth replied and offered him.

'Thanks. I got to get going to the lab. Also, it was a pleasure meeting you. See you,' Ishaan said and offered a handshake.

'No mention dude, can I ask why was he hitting you? Just casually or you asked his sister for a kidney?' Siddharth asked in a funny tone.

'What?' Ishaan giggled, 'No I did not ask for any kidney or stomach,' he paused, 'it wasn't casual either. He just hits me because I am not as cool as him.'

'That's weird man, but hey, our sarcasm level matches, this calls for a Fist-bump. Don't worry man, you got me,' Siddharth said with a grin, 'see you. The class started.'

They parted towards their respective classes.

***

For almost a year, no one thought to hit Ishaan. Who could have? Siddharth was masculine enough to hold two guys with a single hand. But Ishaan never left his side as well. The second part of this story started with ditching classes to teach Siddharth to sneak home to hang out with him. Let's name this part of the story–The HAPPY-ness.

'Sid. can I ask something?' asked Ishaan.

'Go on!' Siddharth replied.

'Why are you so humble and (*He paused*) and so full? Is there something that the world did to you?' Ishaan asked.

After a brief pause, Siddharth collected himself and with a smiling face, 'Yes. The past hasn't been so kind to me. And perhaps, my future is not kind as well. I had a girl in my life, Mugdha. And she was simply beautiful. We were together for almost 3 years and never fought, never cried, and it felt like love, *(He looked towards Ishaan)* initially. Until I realized she was dating my best friend behind me,' he said.

An awkward silence followed. 'Then?' Ishaan asked.

'Then what? I confronted her. And she accepted her double-date game. Both of them were in an intense physical relationship which I wasn't aware of. But that's the boring part,' he replied.

'Umm. What's the interesting one?' Ishaan asked.

'She never regretted it and tried to feel what kind of pain I felt. Truth and loyalty were the only things I deserved. Nothing less and nothing more. *(He was about to cry, he looked at Ishaan)* But you cannot control fate, right?' Siddharth burst into tears.

After a few seconds, 'So, that's that?' Ishaan asked.

'No. In that same month, I was grounded, like falling from a cliff and not dying.' He paused and said in a shivery voice, 'My fate took away my love, my best friend, and a few days later, my father, in a road mishap. (*He sobbed*) and then I couldn't handle this, so I failed my board exams and now, my mom has a cookie business to sustain us both.'

Ishaan was speechless.

'Hey! Chill man. Life is supposed to be like this. It ain't not a damn rainbow, it's greyscale, with more of dark grey. The white part is to be sought,' Siddharth said and paused, 'and that is inevitable.'

Ishaan felt the anguish that Siddharth held but was helpless for his life was smooth and easy.

'You know a hell of a lot of things about life. I mean, my life was quite sorted and easy you know,' Ishaan said, 'I never fell in love, never had a heartbreak, parents supportive, never had money issues, never had a…'

Just as he was about to continue, Siddharth interrupted him and said, 'Dude! If you never got a chance to love, how is your life perfect and sorted without love? In this universe, nothing, absolutely nothing sustains without love. So basically, you have missed out on a very important part of the existence of humankind.'

Ishaan paid close attention to what Siddharth said.

'Maybe your life was not perfect, but just disguised under the blanket of an easy life,' he paused, 'think about it.' Ishaan was confused.

A day later finally, Ishaan realized, his love for Siddharth, and the 'Happy-ness' began.

***

3 months later, Ishaan came out to Siddharth.

'Dude! What? Are you serious right now?' Siddharth asked.

Siddharth was boundlessly happy. He hugged him tightly and exclaimed, 'Dude! I am gay too.'

'Really?' Ishan asked.

'Dhruv!!' Siddharth called and Dhruv entered from the kitchen, 'Here, meet Dhruv, my boyfriend.'

Ishaan was upset on hearing this, he confided his feelings and greeted Dhruv with a smile. The poison that he never deserved to taste, he drank without hesitation for Sid's sake. Neither did he ever mention his feelings. As time went on, the trio started to hang out together.

Siddharth's phone rang while sharing a moment with Dhruv.

'Hello,' he said after ignoring 4 calls.

After 15 seconds, he looked at Dhruv with the call still going on,

'Okay. You better not try to manipulate me,' he said.

Dhruv was curious to know who called.

'Don't worry, I'll be back in just 5 minutes max,' Siddharth said, for the caller called him to meet near his building.

Dhruv was confused. He tried to peep out of the window, seeing Mugdha trying to please Siddharth for a reconciliation. Dhruv panicked.

Siddharth returned with an angry and irritated face.

'Hey, I think I should leave. Got some urgent all from home.' Dhruv said to avoid Siddharth and never called after.

Just when Siddharth thought all is well, a few days later Dhruv left too.

As time progressed, they grew up, Ishaan stayed, to console him at every step, like an umbrella in the rain. Like a shield, he took care of Siddharth. Finally, all was well again when Siddharth decided to love Ishaan. And Ishaan on that very same day, had the first kiss of his life. Ishaan waited for a perfect moment where their families could meet and talk about their future, all he could think of was his birthday. And, everyone met.

'Where are you, Ishaan?' Siddharth asked on a call.

'Just left office, racing in 10, but traffic,' Ishaan said.

'Okay, we are waiting, drive safe,' Siddharth said.

After a while, Ishaan's father got a call from an unknown number saying Ishaan is hit by a car and is admitted to Sayaji Hospital. As they all visited, he was injured badly and collapsed.

Doctors could save him 3 days later, and the family was allowed to meet. Only so Siddharth could see him, he held his hand and started to cry. With the family nearby talking to the doctor, Siddharth realized he has only a few months to live, and he decided to live with Ishaan.

8

Unrequited Love

Shelina Rajawat

We will be lost and found a thousand times along with the cobbled road to us. Like most modern-day love stories, "*He replied to your Instagram story*!" was our starting. I had a broken heart, not ready to open up even a little. Whereas he wanted us to be friends, for me to start talking at least. He was in his training period those days in the Air Force Academy. Well, maybe that's how I saved his name i.e., AFA after his name. He called me every day once he will be done with his everyday training. I once read my poems to him, and he instantly became my fan. Sadly, I used to write previously but had given up on writing thinking I have lost hope for love and that's all I wrote about. Well, I started writing again not like before, but I sat and thought about writing after almost 2 years.

Well, I was in denial mode in the start, scared that I would lose my heart, I had shifted to the new city, and I was a turning introvert. Who would I have talked to? I never wanted to fall in love. But never say never. I was craving to hear his voice every day. Waiting for that one phone call. And as said, what's meant to happen will happen. Trying to be mean, I once agreed to have a call at 2 am and hung up without informing him when I started feeling sleepy. And he was all unaware of this trick, I had just played on him.

We started accepting the fact that we were falling for each other, not openly but through efforts and priorities. Started talking the whole night on weekends, meeting him on his passing out parade, him coming to my city just to meet me. He was gonna pass out soon, and no one was happier than me, but I couldn't show.

I woke up to a picture in the morning, and that was the first time I saw him in uniform, and all my storm came to calm. He is the one, I whispered. I was madly in love with him by then, and I couldn't wait for him to propose to me.

I remember it was 2019, and after he was done with his passing out parade, he was a flying officer now. Our love was reaching heights and I was anxious and scared that it wouldn't work out, what if it broke my heart?

I said, 'I am scared of heights.'

Calmly he replied, 'Come here baby girl, I will save you, I have got wings on my chest.'

THAT WAS THE MOMENT. He proposed and I said yes. That was a moment I can never forget.

He completed all the winding tasks. His parents had come for the POP (Passing Out Parade), and he surely made them proud too. There was documentation that needed to be done, and things that needed to be submitted back, but the birds were free to rely on their wings now. He got done at dawn and took the next bus to Pune. That was the first time he ever travelled on the bus. Being an NCC cadet, had my fell early in the morning, and got back home.

late in the evening. The excitement about meeting your one for the first one had filled both of us with excitement. The moment I got done with the day it was already 10 pm. I lived with my roommates and surely, they knew I was going to meet him the next day. The grooming started, from packing for the next 3-4 days to keeping the best yet comfortable clothes. They all made a playlist of all the love songs popular in those days. We stayed on the video call as the elation of seeing each other after just a few hours kept us awake late.

I woke up with puffy eyes to his call. He was here finally. But on the wrong road. That idiot had turned off his network after turning on the GPS and couldn't find my place. After 20 minutes of making each other understand the current location. And finally, for the first time, I saw him, the face I craved to see for months. The arms that I was longing to be wrapped around, finally he was here. I couldn't believe my eyes still. After a long period of waiting. He was standing at a distance, carrying his basic trek bag and backpack. He was wearing joggers and a T-shirt. But looked all fresh and energetic. That was his aura.

It was December, the peak of winter, and the roads were almost empty, utterly contradictory to our hearts as they were filled with joy and love. Birds were chirping, I woke up 2 hours before me but still, my eyes were equally craving sleep. I normally feel hungry after I wake up and I so was. My sleep, my hunger, my drive to see him, meet him, all of this was so mixed up just like the early morning sun rays and the winter fog was.

Haha! After almost 12 hours of traveling, I made him walk almost 4 km for a cup of tea, which we both didn't like. I still freshly remember the face after the first sip. Then we took a walk around, hand in hand, and he found the lost kid inside of me. My eyes were too shy to look at him and he wouldn't stop looking. We were on the bridge, his arms being my guards, the breeze got my hair tangled, and then caressing my hair moment made it even more romanticized as it does every time in the movies. We watched the sunrise as we both realized, it was more special than we thought. Along with the rising Sun, we could feel our love rising and getting brighter and brighter as it rose.

Then after a while, we checked into the hotel, I was so impressed by how he signed. Just as smooth as he was in wooing me. We honestly did not care how the room was but just for the sake of courtesy, yes it was so nice. We went for adventure rides, where I was always up for experiencing breathtaking rides and he was both excited and scared at the same time. Whenever he felt scared, he used to hold my hand so tight that the kid inside me enjoyed it. The drive from the hotel and the amusement park was an adventurous ride in itself as we drove to Lonavala on a two-wheeler.

We went on a dinner date, both all dressed up and looking pretty. We were so into each other that we did not care much about the food or the service there, but I hope it was pretty good. After that, we came back to our room, all tired and just wanted to get into his arms and cuddle. We were soaked into each other's arms where I slept first and then he did, I guess.

The next morning, I woke up to the sight of his sleepy face and it felt like, "Yes! This is what I want to see when I wake up every morning from now on."

It was so refreshing and serene that I woke up first and got ready, for a change. Haha! Then we went out for a morning walk in the cold and dawning setup. We grabbed something for breakfast on our way back and had coffee in our room and talked till we got ready.

As time passed by both did not know. There's a saying in Hindi *"Acche waqt ki ek burai yeh hai ke woh jaldi khatam ho jata hai.* (The thing about happy times is, they slip fast)" And that was about to get real pretty soon.

It felt like a demo (you know if you know) of my whole life in three. What life is going to be with him, around him? After a very long time, I was so sure about what I wanted in life and was so delighted and equally nervous about it. I knew he was "the one" for me. We were so much better together and every moment we spent was proof of that.

And finally, it was the moment he was leaving, I realized the sadness a couple of days after his departure. My heart started aching for his arms. My eyes started craving that one glance of him. My mind wanted him to be there for me all the time. And all these feelings went on getting stronger because somewhere I knew that he was not going to be there all the time. Destiny and time would make me wait for a text from him to pop up in my notifications. Calls, meetings, and being around him were tough. Even when you have fights, they would either be solved due to lack of communication or will be continued in the next episode of our conversation series. Well, that's ironic and funny. Loving him made everything so easy and smooth though.

Well, this is your story when you are dating a soldier. Long days of no meeting, different cities most of the time of the year, just a couple of days together in a year. But trust me, it's worth it. They are worth the wait. That first sight of him was worth every moment of waiting and missed festivals. Every second that I spent thinking about him, I cried. I so wanted him to come back and spend at least one minute with me if possible and I would be smiling until our next meeting. I was lonely but with him. I was vulnerable at times but that part of me was just for us to handle and take care of. What he was with him took all the pain.

The next few months went swiftly, it was March, and he was posted to Rajasthan for training. He was not allowed to share many of the details with me. Patience is the only thing that kept me going. Waiting for his one text or call was an integral part of my life and yes it was hard but worth it. That was the time when destiny played its part, I didn't know that was just our story. Just that. He was there for a good time not for a long time. I promised I will always love him and will do, whether he is there to watch on me or not.

Twelve years down the line, my heart still aches every day for him. The hope of his soul being around me keeps me alive.

9

To Destiny, via Love

Varun Sargwan

Ada hastily recollected her thoughtful mind and heart, just a moment before assembling a few loosened white sheets of paper and her closest companion, an ink pen. A yellow umbrella, which seemed to contrast against the white-painted Himalayas, the erected pine, and the melodious Jhelum, offered a substantial shed.

A smog of emotions embraced her now. Her oozing tears emulated the raindrops, except the former had more feelings than the mere water. Lakshya had not stopped picturing before her hazel eyes. She often cursed her unreceptive mind for their miserable departure. But Lakshya had always known it was not her fault, and the perception she owned was the outcome of her personal experience ever since she could sense things.

'Lakshya, I will hand over a list, get these items in the evening,' said his mom.

'You people have wasted my youth in these household things,' said Lakshya in a rebellious tone. But at the end of the day, 'Lakshya, do you want kheer or halwa as a dessert today?' Mom asked.

'Mom it was so delicious,' was his statement at the end of the day.

Lakshya was a typical Scorpion, filled with a heightened level of principles. The eyes coal-black envisaged colourful thoughts. Emotions fused with passion intoxicated him seldom. His thirst for a better human often separated him from conventional society.

Till now, he had only one dream–The Indian Army. He was enthralled by the army so much that even after being knocked out six times by the army interview panel, he murmured *"Jab Tak Hai Jaan!"* (As Long as I Live).

In Srinagar, J&K, 'Grandma, just sit and relax,' Ada said as she sat beside her finest companion with two mugs, semi-filled with *kahwa* (a traditional Kashmiri tea). For hours, the duo relaxed on the balcony, relishing the flickered sunlight that came through restless chinar leaves, only to massage their body. The winters in exile had started stretching back to their homeland.

Ada, a future doctor, had to pull out of medical college due to a grave ailment. She was now an undergraduate with a fist-size dream and myriad smiles on her milky face. Practicality ran down her veins while arteries transited etiquettes. Her preferred time pass was her granny, with whom she was living away from her parents. Life circled college, friends, and granny with a pinch of internet blended.

'Ahhh! Who the hell is not faking in these chat rooms?' Lakshya murmured as the dying net signed him out.

'I should not waste Papa's money for my fun, but let's give it one last try,' he uttered, and the poking started.

Ada was not a night owl; a few minutes of online chit-chat with college friends were enough to douse her dehydrating tongue. She rushed the cursor over a prompt window deeming it was them. 'Hello,' a stranger poked. She overlooked. 'Hi ma'am,' prompted yet again. No one had ever addressed her as ma'am on chats. Her curiosity pressure built up, and the 'chat' wrapped up in a short period with both added to their list.

The duo turned excited over their new acquaintances. However, Ada retained tranquillity. Lakshya popped up online and kept waiting. The girl tested his patience for a while. Ada, not being so outspoken, mostly kept silent and let Lakshya babble. The boy's firm belief in honesty prompted him to let sail A-Z things about himself. But Ada kept the maximum word with her, letting flow only location, and profession—a medical student from Kashmir, and her parents are currently in Australia, thus staying with her granny. Lakshya's heart squeezed a bit as the parent's location got disclosed. 'Oho!!! Some rich girls she is. Might not match my standards,' murmured his heart.

With their daily e-coffees, Lakshya assumed that, possibly, Ada has inclined toward him. And one day, he proposed to her. The dumb guy had kept the persuasion on a high note, even after a series of obvious NOs. It was a green signal from her. He was so silly that once, proposed to her to be in a relationship for a week's probation. Their future could then be decided by his performance. So, one day, everything happened as it happens in typical movies.

Ada's confession list elongated with this white lie of *falling in love*. For her, it was a wise woman's guilt she carried. She grew addicted to him but never crossed the hairline margin that segregated friendship and love. She was often amazed at Lakshya's blind love for her without the want of her single snap. So, the wise woman thought heavily, blew away the white lie, and proposed for an uncomplicated but stable friendship only.

"Beggars are not choosers." Lakshya preserved the special friend status. The flowerbed of chat blossomed. He had no in-time or out-time, while the girl's out-time was marked at midnight, owing to the midnight power cut, except on Saturdays. Whose studies, whose dinner? The boy had plunged deeper into emotions now. One day his father yelled at him for dining with the computer daily.

Ada now had numerous things to discuss, but comparatively less than what Lakshya had to.

“Ada_123 sends scan001.jpg”

“Accept or Reject?”

Several questions fired inside the boy as this caught his eye.

‘Wow!! Not a bad choice,’ Lakshya, with a self-satisfied smile. He could not realize this reticence passed on her snap. But an exact snap as wallpaper on a college friend’s cell came up as a firm slap.

‘This girl is famous on the net,’ replied his friend with a dirty smile.

As Ada clarified, trusting some alien blindly was not her trait.

‘I was once a medical student, but now a general science undergraduate, and at this stage, it is enough for you to know this,’ said a puzzled Ada. Lakshya in the grip of love, could not act as was desired. He fused a moral lecture with a tough tone.

With the end of Ada’s ongoing exam, one life had ceased to breathe. An entire week had squeezed tears from her “hazel eyes”, which had now sunken deep in the memories.

Lakshya, on New Year’s Eve, returned from Mussoorie with his friends. But his heart had pinched continuously the entire day at Ada’s longest-ever break. There was no reply to his offline messages too.

His eyes focused on the messenger, “My granny is no more,” appeared a message, and then the broken girl popped online.

Lakshya at once kept aside all the excitement. He by now had known the granny’s significance in Ada’s life.

‘How are you?’ asked Lakshya.

“How could I be?’ Ada asked after a pause.

She knew he was trying to fill the void, but the shattered emotions pierced her back quite hard. Over the next few days, an alien shoulder turned out to be her comfort space.

One evening Ada confessed the biggest ever lie to him. She, for sure, lived with her granny, but her parents were neither doctors nor settled in Australia. Her family resided in Srinagar. To take care of her lone granny she had shifted there, and now it was time to return home. Ada knew these indigestible lies would end everything between Lakshay and her.

Lakshya smiled and said, 'I like you for the genuineness of your emotions over various instances till now. Not for some facts about you. They don't describe you. And I understand how careful a girl needs to be.'

No doubt, a layer of trust was added.

'You'll surely adore the route on the lap of the Himalayas–Jammu to Srinagar. But why are you visiting a place always subdued by guns?' asked a confused Ada.

Lakshya had chosen Srinagar as an exam center; the feeling of being in J&K alone was inexplicable.

"This is where I wish for my foremost posting after joining the army," murmured his heart.

Finally, the exam and a flight over the white Himalayas locked up the experience in his mind. The trip pumped in more trust in Ada.

"This guy is unique in thoughts and is charming," she thought to herself, gazing at his snap.

Shyly, she confessed her love before him.

The duo spent some quality time now. Both focused more on each other than on any trivial topic. While Lakshya would ferry her through a fantasy world, it was Ada's charisma that showered unmatched peace on him. Post Lakshya's Kashmir trip, the duo drew them into the Kashmir riddle. He vocally advocated Kashmiris' right to lead a peaceful life. His keenness to join the armed forces was reflected now. Ada did not approve of his dream much. Her every teardrop had a story to tell; how loathed these military people were.

Lakshya did not try to prove her wrong, for he knew some events had been etched in her memory. Pissed between the two obsessions, he left it to be resolved later and never let such a subject erupt again.

A few months later, the profound joy of selection in the army was overshadowed by the mind swinging amid Ada and the army. He waited for the final merit and call letter. Till then, Ada was not let to hear the beats of joy and distress in his heart.

After being poked for not appearing online, he revealed to her the whole episode of being an under-training Gentleman Cadet at the prestigious Indian Military Academy. To their helplessness, both cried. Ada could not move on from what she had experienced and already accepted that he would one day become one of those blindfolded humans on a rampage. She often stayed depressed and argued with him frequently.

Ada felt, "Love is not always holding on to the partner. Sometimes letting go is the best possibility."

Slowly the love faded to acquaintances, and eventually, everything was limited to just the good old days.

***

Srinagar

Immediately, Lakshya tallied the snap in his wallet with what he had seen seconds before.

'Oh, my God! I love this place,' he shouted with joy from his core.

Ada had walked past an army post on the other side of the road with lowered eyes. Lieutenant Lakshya stood in charge of that site in central Srinagar. Daily she passed, and not a single day he missed adoring her. Not to burden her agile mind again, he refrained from any contact and observed her from a distance. Ada noticed him a day and cautiously remained out of his sight. She felt guilty for washing off the trust. Now, as she passed over any army post, her eyes explored every corner to locate Lakshya.

Then, a day their sight froze on each other. Tears found their way. The eyes revived what had not been lost, the buffered love. Now, they talked daily over calls and met whenever feasible.

On one grey morning roared not clouds but gunfire. There was a hostage crisis in the city outskirts, and Lakshya was attached to the operation. The operation swallowed a life.

As the news dispersed, Ada grew restive. She started murmuring prayers. But soon, the televised report confirmed an officer casualty. A bullet had breached Lakshya's stomach as he evacuated a child. The shock soaked in all her tears.

What flowed from her heart was, "You remained unique throughout. I should have trusted you."

For months ahead, Ada could not get hold of her life. Piercing more into the memories, she conceded to herself, "How her stern belief system eroded the best time of her life with Lakshya. In the battle of the mind, and heart why did she let the mind win?"

Her sobbing heart thought, "Life is beautifully sculpted to endure pain, heal, fight darkness, rebuild, and celebrate the moments bestowed. We knit complexities around and adore getting entangled. In the process, we fail to swim across the precious moments. We forget to unchain ourselves from regret and guilt consumed over the years."

Ada's moist eyes recollected the pieces of her immortal love and never let anyone know about it. She got married, attained motherhood, and lived a blissful life. The bliss, she realized, was the outcome of her self-discovery as a stranger, a friend, and a lover to Lakshya. She made peace!

10

The Jinxed 'Love Affair'

Nadeem Shah

(Warning: Cigarette smoking is injurious to health)

Sajad lit a cigarette, turned his head, and blew the noxious smoke over his shoulder. It wasn't the "normal" behavior that we had become accustomed to with him. Whenever he smoked, he puffed the air towards whosoever was sitting nearer to him much to the person's annoyance. But, today, something was amiss, and we could sense it. He had a forlorn look on his face and was unusually quiet. We were sitting under the shades of the majestic Chinars in the Jhelum View Park on a hot Sunday afternoon; the sun was spewing fire.

Lava was simmering inside Sajad, waiting for the right moment to burst out and relieve his bosom. And after suppressing the urge to pour his heart out in front of his friends, for so long, he finally gave up and blurted out: *Tamis ha karekh nishean raath*. Instead of getting any sympathetic words, he received a burst of loud laughter. We burst into guffaws, much to the astonishment of the passersby, and Sajad himself couldn't fight back a faint smile. After we were done, we wondered if the import of his words dawned on us. All of us felt sorry for Sajad, for our inappropriate behavior and there was silence all around.

This wasn't the first time that Sajad had faced such a disappointment though. In the recent past, two more girls had slipped through his hands, and he was left dejected and alone. On one occasion he had even served *Wazwan* (a multi-course meal in Kashmiri cuisine) at the marriage ceremony of his ex who tied the knot to her cousin working in Dubai. The next time he fell for a girl, destiny played its tricks again and the girl got engaged to an NRK within six months of the affair. His recent relationship didn't last six months either. The girl in question again went into the share of a Kashmiri Doctor based in America. It would have been wrong to blame Sajad, had he developed an entrenched disdain for all the foreign-based Kashmiri professionals. But, instead of brooding over the "bad experiences" of his past, he shrugged off these incidents and resolved to try his luck again.

Every single guy, other than me, in our friend circle of "Daydreamers" had a poignant story to share.

Arif's ex-girlfriend, whose name sounded somewhat similar to the opposite of Zameen, got engaged to a guy who exported carpets. His new catch was Rosy, whom he affectionately called Rose. Arif would have drowned in the sea of his Rose's love, just like Jack Dawson in Titanic, except that there now stood her fiancé, her cousin, between them like an iceberg.

Ishaq's love interest from Pattan reportedly eloped with a truck driver. It was difficult to cajole Amir into spilling his secret but there were rumours that the girl he loved, was betrothed during our University days when Amir had cast his evil eye on her. Amir loved the girl intensely, but he didn't have the guts to propose to her.

After my friends' recurring setbacks in love, we concluded that we are a cursed group; that we are destined to stay bachelors forever. We often amuse ourselves by suggesting that we should open a matrimonial consultancy. Our bad luck would have earned us a lot of fortune, paradoxically. The modus operandi was simple: An unmarried girl registers with us and chooses anyone among us, or all of us, as a boyfriend(s) depending on her level of desperation to get married; wait till six months for the curse to do its job; 50 percent money-back guarantee. Why just half rebate, you ask? Because 50 percent will be spent on tea and coffee charges in the swanky restaurants so that the couple gets the real feel of the 'affair'.

As far as I was concerned, I was reluctant to fall in love; so, there was no chance of the curse affecting me. Or maybe I thought it wasn't my cup of tea. Then "she" happened, and my world turned upside down.

Let's name her "B" (because A is too banal and clichéd). B was a feisty girl who lived, let's say, in Florida. In the recent past a world-renowned Puppet Master, Jewbin Behta, had conducted a puppet show in the famed garden of Florida. The natives had declared the show a failure because they were the only ones who were not allowed inside the premises. I too was outraged! Back to the story! Miss Florida worked in an NGO named IGSTU that got its funding through the Hawala system.

B would invariably laugh at her jokes and the drop of a hat. She was a person who would express her hearty laugh at a funeral, instead of heartfelt condolences.

I met B through our mutual friends, and she seemed interested in me from the very beginning. I received WhatsApp messages and Pokes, but I was impervious. She made advances that I duly thwarted with utter heartlessness. I ridiculed and mocked her in front of everyone to the point of driving her mad. But she wouldn't give up and pursued me with the same vigour and zeal that she had exhibited the first time we had met. I had no inkling, though, that the tide would turn eventually, and I would fall head-over-heels in love with the same girl whose face I couldn't stand the sight of.

On hot summer Sundays, as the taps in our homes ran dry, we would rush to a nearby stream, tear off our clothes and dive into its ice-cold waters. The stream lies two kilometres beyond Florida.

On one fine day, my friend Suhaib and elder brother Waseem decided a day out at our favorite haunt, our piece of paradise where the drooping branches of the Weeping Willows fell into the stream. We piled into the car and sped away. I was sitting in the rear relishing my pack of chips and coke, when I suddenly realized we were passing through Florida. I peep out the window to find a familiar-looking figure coming from the opposite direction. It was "her"; draped in green shalwar and black headscarf that accentuated her fair countenance. But what struck me today was the look of defeat and dejection wearing on her usually happy and cheerful face. She seemed to be in a dismal state; like she had been through the worst day of her life. She didn't see me, but I followed her with my eyes till our car took a turn at the curve, and I lost her.

Our titular hero in the brilliant drama series "Sherlock" says, LOVE IS A DANGEROUS DISADVANTAGE. Those words began to make sense somehow at that instant. My feelings about B were beginning to change and I could do nothing to stop them. We reached our destination, but I couldn't bring myself to jump into the stream. I feigned illness and watched the duo splash water on each other.

Back at home, I recalled every insult I had heaped on her. I felt a mixture of guilt, shame, and embarrassment. I wanted to hold her in a tight embrace, no, just hold her hand and seek her forgiveness for every indignity I had doled out to her. I hadn't been so depressed after watching Mughal-e-Azam, as I felt on that day. But it was useless to cry over the spilled milk that was laced with the cement of indifference and the fertilizer of contempt.

That night after some vain efforts to sleep, I ended up tossing and turning till the streaks of sunlight fell into my room. I woke up and made a firm resolve to set everything right and tell her how apologetic I was. I just had to wait for her next WhatsApp message and make my move.

Meanwhile, the desperation set in, and I would pluck a rose from our garden every morning and pocket it carefully. But our paths didn't cross for a long time and soon the garden was conspicuously and mysteriously left desolate much to my grandmom's shock and dismay.

On a typical lazy morning, I received a message, it was her, I replied from atop cloud nine. I didn't want to squander this chance and greeted her with utmost kindness much to her bewilderment. And soon began the continuous round of chatting that only ended the time our batteries gave up.

I had felt so much joy in someone's company for the first time in my life. Whenever I saw her, my heartbeat went through the roof (if we met indoors). Her name sounded music to my ears, and I longed every moment for her glimpse.

But my joy was short-lived. Instead of blossoming, our 'relationship' ran into some rough weather over trivial age issues. She was two years older than me and that was a major concern for her. I snubbed her for her "age obsession" but she was unmoved.

Whenever she pointed to the "difference in our age", I would hit back by reminding her superiority of the imposing physique that I enjoyed over her. Occasionally, I would tease her by saying: I have three strands of grey hair on my head, so who is older now?

I was growing frustrated with her and wanted to shut her out. But I realized she liked me so much that she didn't want to be a part of my life. Then the worst tragedy struck Kashmir and communication networks collapsed. For many days I didn't even try to reach her even though she sent an odd message to which I didn't care to reply.

A semblance of normalcy returned after the devastating floods but by then she had faded out of my life. Weeks passed and I began to have a strange premonition. Finally, when I logged in to my Facebook account, I saw my worst fears come true. She had updated her Relationship from Single to Engaged. It was the shock of a lifetime. I closed my eyes fearing the tears might well up in them and said to myself,

THE CURSE LIVES ON.

11

The Cryptic Path

Mahek Thakar

Nia stood in the frost with a frozen heart. She was as still as a statue but somewhere within that storm, that volcano tried its best to burst out, which she never allowed to erupt. Her feminine tenderness took the place of harsh deep wounds, and she became as wrathful as fire. The railing which she held with her right hand led her to her fondest hometown. Soon she dived deep into the sweetest memory of her life, where she smelled the typical smell of her small and most loved hometown. She remembered the children shouting her name for playing. Now all the neighbourhood friends, were about to complete their high school studies and looking for the best college for their specific streams. In everyday meetings, the discussions went on. She could hear the human voices in that dead silence of snowbound winter. From those voices, a baritone gentle voice came out and met her ear. She became more conscious to hear it. Slowly she was sinking deep down into her memories so that she could find the reason for her existence which had a robust connection with that special voice.

Rajveer was a tall, dark, handsome, and intelligent guy and most importantly Nia's manly friend. She was too a feminine yet courageous and adventurous girl whose mind was as vast as the sky, and only a boy like Rajveer could be that sky for her, in which she can fly endlessly. The companionship itself begins by showing and playing manly fortes, bike rides, and talks about free living, music, and career sides, in short, it was a "Buddyness" between a boy and a girl. It was not at all an ordinary bond. Gradually it bloomed beautifully with the water of honesty and trust.

It was the year 2003. The cool breeze of a soothing calm summer evening was touching Nia's soft pink cheeks as she stood tenderly at a corner of the terrace. She could see Rajveer sitting on the compound wall, waiting for his father to drop him off at the railway station. After many deliberations between his parents and Nia, finally, it was decided that he would go to Bengaluru for his further studies. Of course, it was a hard decision for all as he was leaving his hometown, his family, and his buddies behind. This was the very fresh start of his first term. It was 9 at night and he had to catch his train scheduled to depart at 10. There was still an hour left. His small bag pack was lying beside him, and he was sitting at his favored routine place (on the small compound wall) from where he could see Nia standing in front of him on her terrace. This was the spot where their eyes met just at a glance and spoke more than a thousand words. Waving hands by gazing at each other was their unique way to say, "I will miss you, study well and come back soon in holidays." In this way, their hearts had just started connecting with the same frequency.

Like Rajveer, Nia also wanted to study at a good campus, so she also got admission to IIT Kanpur. To communicate with each other, they often used the public telephone. They decided on a particular day every month to call and share the happenings of their campus life. The sharing went on and the time came to introduce their crushes. Both were very excited to meet each other's heartthrobs. All four people met at a multi-cuisine eating joint where Nia and Rajveer seemed happier and more eager to share than Ananya and Rahul. Both were mature enough to look after their love so that they don't feel aloof. It became worth spending the evening as the four of them met and read colourful dreams in each other's eyes.

All the intentions were good, and circumstances were in favor too, but it perhaps did not assent to fate. Rajveer almost emotionally collapsed when Ananya broke apart the relationship without any reason. It was not at all acceptable and he failed last semester. He thought he would not share this sorrowful news with Nia as it would hurt her, and she would argue with Ananya regarding their breakup. So, he just called up Nia as usual and shared about other stuff. On the other hand, Nia also refused to share that she is consulting a shrink. She lost her mind when Rahul deceived her and just vanished. He did not come back for the last 3 months, and each passing day was a burden on her. Finally, she couldn't make up for herself and she had to consult a shrink. When both Rajveer and Nia came to know about each other their bond even became discerning.

Was this the turning point of their life? Or a jerk of triggering love inside?

Rajveer was a practical and logical lover. He had a soft corner for Nia, who was spiritual and sensible, a keen believer in love and destiny, and most importantly who worshiped love as God. It was very hard for Nia to accept the proposal from Rajveer just because she never wanted to lose a genuine relationship with him. It took some time to realize but finally, their love story went well. Nia had completely accepted Rajveer; he was everything to her. She felt as if their souls were directly connected. But all she regretted, was the timing. Their love was unique. It was beyond the earthly explanations. She always felt their love heightened her life. For the love was in the air. Then what happened?

Did the marriage bells ring & the lovely love story come to an end?

A decade passed ...

With a long furry woollen overcoat and winter boots, Nia was standing at the frosty lake shore. Her heart was frozen like the waters of Lake Abraham. It was the climax of her patience which she had been holding for ages. She was as still as a statue but somewhere within that storm, that volcano was making its best efforts to burst out, which she never allowed to rise. Her feminine tenderness took the place of harsh deep wounds, and she became as wrathful as fire. Each limb of her body was shouting out loud for Rajveer. She wanted justice for her life. This was the only aim left for her. To her surprise, her prayers were finally answered. Her heart skipped a beat when the cell phone beeped. Suddenly her body started shivering as if she felt Rajveer's presence. Alas! It was severely cold in Alberta. She couldn't figure out the rapid change in each of each body cells, something ran very fast into the nerves. It became very difficult for her to control their body, immediately she held the railing with her right hand and all her past came alive in a blink of an eye, like it wanted to convey it was not all Rajveer's fault. His heart and his love were as pure as hers. Even the message from Rajveer explaining his crucial situations in life and fulfilling Nia's dream of becoming an author (he wrote a novel that depicted their love) conveyed the same. And at the end, Nia got relieved and liberated, since her love came home as a quote by Rumi goes,

You cannot hide love.

Love will get on its way.

To the heart of someone you love

Far or near, it goes home.

To where it belongs

To the heart of lovers.

12

A Voiceless Goodbye

Vanitha Murugan

Justin

Justin Snow prepared for his usual morning. A cup of coffee on a verdant balcony could raise some ideas about his new book.

Ivy vines immersed with dewy mist; extra hot coffee compensated for the freezing climate.

'There will be a dozen emails within these two days which should be replied to soon or else I'd even lose my existing readers. The phone has been in DND mode.'

'Oh, my God! 20 missed calls from– Sweet Poison.'

'I don't know why she called me multiple times. She is going to kill me. There is no way to run away from her chides.'

'Yeah, I shall call her, there's no choice.'

Lucy

'Why hasn't he called still?'

'I called him after ages, I miss him so much!'

Lucy Vargas spent her holiday at her grandparent's house even though she didn't want to spend her vacation with the grey-haired elders. However, she couldn't refuse. Her parents are like army-trained people with a list of rules and rude personalities. Sometimes she would weep in pain, the things which can comfort her are Justin's warm caresses and sweet love towards her. They met in their sophomore year while practicing for a college cultural festival.

Lucy's phone pings.

'He might be the one calling me. Yeah, it's him.'

A broad smile on my face, and a yearning to hear his voice made me emotional.

He apologized for not responding to my calls.

I didn't want his apologies, I only wanted to hear his voice throughout the day, his hands caressing my cheeks and our giggling. I want his warm love which I missed in the past two days. I just ignored his apologies and just started hearing his voice, I adored his voice like this was the first time I heard his voice message over my phone.

He stopped talking and asked me why I was being silent since he started talking. I said I missed him like hell.

Justin

She told me that she missed me. And I just smiled back because I didn't see it coming. I've also missed her. I couldn't pass my day without her stupid jokes, craziness, and entirely inside my arms. I told her about the beginning of the new book. She was happy about it and offered her help to not disturb me. I appreciated that. It'll help me to be completely awash in my new writing. I'll go and meet her when I feel like finished half of my ideas. Yeah, spending time with her relishes me.

I finished my cup of coffee and started my work. In between the publishing company called me to enlighten me about the deadline for my work. I have to finish it soon or else I'd vanish into the commoner's air.

I wanted to write an emotional love story. I have no ideas blossoming in my mind.

Lucy

Lucy has to do the chores; she watered the plants in their garden. Lucy's father summoned her. She has to follow up on everything, including their parents' wishes. The last thing she wants to do is listen to them for everything they order for.

Instead of getting irritated with my parents, I sprinkled water on plants with a pristine broad grin. He is the one who makes me smile every time he talks.

'Why am I still blushing? Oh God, he is such a cutesy boyfriend. I am dying for embracing all his love.'

'I want to take a glance at him as soon as he finishes his book and also, I forgot that it's Megan's birthday!'

When she saw me, she was on cloud 9. We girls just rocked the night, and I wasn't sleeping because something struck my mind. Yeah, it was the gift Megan got from her boyfriend. He didn't come to her party because of his full-time job in Canada, he just surprised her virtually. She was whirled into joyous tears to see him. It was such a beautiful scene that happened today.

'I wanted to give Justin the same, joyous tears. But I don't know if he would cry or just laugh at my face for being soppy.'

'When I get back, I will give him a small surprise visit.'

Justin

Justin was blanked midway. He needs some help from his college senior Myla Berenson.

'I need some help from someone well-versed in literature.'

I took the phone and scrolled down to the name Myla. She'll help me to get back into the stream. I was going to call Myla.

But there comes a call from my sweet poison.

'It is Lucy's.'

I didn't answer her call.

Then I pinged Myla and asked her if she could come and help me with some lines.

She was very happy to help.

'I can call Lucy after this book gets finished. Now I must focus on my lines.'

The doorbell rings. I rushed to the door, and it was Myla. She had changed a lot. I invited her in. She seemed to be excited. She apologized for her delay. I thanked her for stopping by, I told her the problems about being blank and stocking with some lines. She helped me throughout the things which I had written that day. I was not in the mood to go out with her, so I brewed some coffee for her.

We just talked a lot about our college days. I laughed a lot after months. Suddenly, my front door creaked. It was Lucy who opened the door. She just saw us laughing together and just bolted out of the house. I know she must be angry for ignoring her calls.

'I have to let go of whatever happens. My writing should be the first thing that I have to bother about.'

It's been six months; I finally completed my novel with the help of Myla. She has been the one who helped me out with the entire book. Lucy didn't interfere after that day. I didn't try to explain to her. I hope she will understand my situation. Tomorrow is a big day when she will never forget to call. I'll just explain to her later. I missed her but couldn't call her because there was a load of work.

'This night will be a calm one for me because I can finally make time for Lucy. I can see the moon smiling with brilliance, wishing me my beautiful day tomorrow.'

I woke up to the smell of coffee, sure it was my mother. There was a coffee with a note wishing me for my precious years ahead. I didn't expect that mom would leave such a cute note. It was a blissful morning. I wanted to see Lucy right away. I just jumped out of my bed. I wanted to give Mom a tight hug, but I have no idea where she had gone. The doorbell rang and I bolted to open the door.

'It has to be Lucy. When I see her, I'm just gonna kiss her until I feel like enough.'

There was a big box I hoped that Lucy had brought this. But it wasn't Lucy. It was a tall man with a cap bearing a postal service badge. When my mom arrived, I opened that box. It was a canvas portrait. I couldn't believe my eyes. It was the last picture of me and my dad, taken just two days before his death. Me and my mom broke down in tears. That picture had always kept me strong in every situation. It was majestic. I couldn't ably see it clearly because of my tears-filled blurry eyes.

I comforted my mom and read the note which was glued back to the portrait.

Hey babe, I hope you have seen this portrait.

I tried to paint this, but you know, I suck at art.

I don't wanna spoil this, so asked a friend to do this magical portrait for you.

And this was not for you to cry, whenever you see this, you have to be strong like you were during the time with your dad.

He'll be happy when you succeed in everything you lead with your rigid unbreakable heart.

Hey man, look at the portrait one person is missing.

And it's your Lucy, so prepare a portrait for my cute stupid face.

I'll be waiting for it, and I accept it even if you suck at it.

And I nearly forgot that one thing.

"Happy birthday baby"

Love,

Lucy (THE SWEET POISON)

My red puffy eyes were then filled with gallons of tears. Yet, my lips grinned because of the way she asked me to paint for her.

'Yeah dear, you are my sweet poison indeed. Making me cry and smile at the same time. Where are you at this time? I need your shoulders to hold my head. I want to weep over your lap.'

And again, the doorbell rings. I opened the door to just hug Lucy. It's not her but a bunch of people wishing me. I just wanted to see her face in that crowd. Just go towards her and hold her hands.

They asked me to come to my garden where a big white screen was mounted. My mom followed me to the garden. They asked me to sit on a chair to see the video playing on the screen.

In the video, it was her in a hospital, surrounded by beeping machines. She looked skinny and dull.

'What the hell happened to her? I couldn't glance at her like this.'

There comes a familiar voice talking to me in the video.

Happy birthday my dear

I hope you've got your portrait gift.

Haven't you started painting yet?

'Oh my god, what the hell is happening? Her voice is so low, I'm not used to her talking this low.'

You may wonder what happened to me.

This is just a medical condition dear. Don't worry I'll be alright.

I am not sure if I will be there when this video reaches you.

Just ask the man who is behind you wearing specs whether I survived this or not.

I glanced at the man she told, he just held his head down and it meant she was no more.

'I don't know what's happening here.'

My chest got heavy. I couldn't breathe, I could feel my breath getting shallow. My swollen eyes shed tears. My eyes refused to open. I'm afraid of what's she gonna talk about next. I don't want to hear more. It's hurting. I'm going to collapse. I could feel my legs trembling and my whole body getting numb.

She continued to talk.

Sorry for causing you dismay during your birthday. I tried calling you, but my heart refused to disturb you while you progress in writing.

Whenever my head feels like exploding, I want to call you,

I don't want a nurse or doctor looking after me every time I get aches in my head.

I only needed you to hold my hands and cuddle into your arms.

I just wanted to spend my last hours with you.

Even though I don't want my parents near me,

I just need your warmth to hold my soul.

I want to rest my soul over your lap hearing your voice.

I don't want you to feel guilty.

I'm just sharing my life when you weren't there.

Just live your life to the fullest, Justin.

I want you to succeed in your writing stream.

My boy, write a novel about me, okay?

Whatever happens,

I love you always and forever.

Once again HAPPY BIRTHDAY my man

You're always mine.

'No, no, no, no!!'

'This shouldn't be happening; I want to see her face.'

I wanted to scream.

'Lucy, where are you? Just show me your face.'

Justin screamed. His legs trembled and he collapsed.

There she is, behind the screen there was a big gift box. I can see her getting out of the box. It's a surprise, she just wanted to surprise me. Yeah, it's her, she is alive. Thank God, my baby is here. My heart is pounding. I just pulled her into my arms.

'I don't wanna breathe, I just want to hug you tightly. I won't leave you this time.'

She was perfectly all right, and she just acted for the video to make me cry. I thought that was true. It didn't happen. I just wanted her in my arms.

'I won't leave you this time for sure.'

Some voices whispered around me.

My mom called me aloud.

I heard 'Justin, darling, you collapsed!'

Suddenly I opened my eyes, I was still in my garden covered by the same bunch of people. But I needed that one person to wake me up. But she wasn't there.

'Yeah, she wasn't here. She was dead.'

'I want to say goodbye to her at least.

No one should suffer this pain, I couldn't even hear her last words, hold her hand and give her a proper goodbye. I should have gone behind her that day. I should have focused on my Lucy also.

She even planned a surprise for me during her last days.

I lost that only person who cared and loved me more than herself.

'I love you and I miss you, Lucy. Please forgive me,' my voiceless heart screamed.

My voiceless heart screamed, helplessly as she departed.

13

In an Unparallel Universe

Prerna Dhingra

Dreams they say are very powerful. They are hopeful and full of colours as a peacock's feather. But when broken, break a part of you. It shatters you to the extent that your colourful canvas slowly turns greyscale.

Love is beautiful, they say, but it is both chaos and peace. It's a like a series of painful covid vaccination, beneficial to your health but bringing in pain.

How often do we hope for hope when the dreams shatter? Do we associate love with anything except failed metaphors? My story is no different, it is just mine. A truth greater than fiction. A story whose characters are unnamed because of the relationship we shared, failed to fit into either defined roles penned by society. He was my everything, yet not mine. He wanted to be mine, but he couldn't. We were like the ocean and the sky, which seemed to meet at the horizon but did not. We were the old poem, with the poet trying his best to complete it. A constant battle of victory of fate over free will. It felt like the lines on my palm were untraceable, just like a web.

I boarded the train and struggled with my extra luggage. I was advised by my mother to carefully handle my luggage as they had fragile items, made up of her love, for a part of her heart was going on a work tour to Chandigarh. I somehow settled myself and those bags, waiting for my co-occupant. I glared out of the window and felt unsettled. I seemed to have an existential crisis thinking if changing places would change my life! There was something in me that made me loosely hang hopes to a monotonous work tour. Disturbing my thoughts, there was a knock at the door. There came a face that was familiar to me more than anything, a face I could read and hear without words, the eyes whose misery I had shared, the hair I had touched, the lips that I had kissed. I still carried a part of him with me. The eyes had the same pain, and the lips seemed to utter my name but were so overwhelmed that they failed to do so. It's been ages since I had seen him or heard of him. His appearance looked more mature, with serious spectacles and a round beard. It was hard for me to believe that it was him! Words seem to forget their way inside my vocal cord, they were lost somewhere! I struggled to connect with the network at this broken cord of communication. My eyes, however, were my ally and couldn't stop the humble flow of tears. I gathered all my courage and screamed his name. My name from his lips seemed to be the drug my soul had been craving for the past few years.

The train from New Delhi to Chandigarh seemed to be a paradox. My destiny crossed paths with the man I always wished to unite with, yet our fates never synced. This was nothing but a ray of hope, for someone who has given up on love. Little did I know where this journey would lead me to. If crossing my path with him was a signal that it was the right time or to completely shatter my will to love. Seeing him, my heart and mind raced into a series of flashbacks. All that came to my mind was that dream, where I dreamt of sharing a home with him; a lavish garden, and a cushion macrame swing on my balcony sipping tea. The lazy devil in me asked him to let me wake up late, while old school romantic in him asked me to wake him up every morning with a cup of tea. After every discussion, to my astonishment, he would complete my incomplete sentences. He was the first love of my life and I had intended him to be the last as well. He was the solace of the temple, the serenity of the mountains, the calmness of the seas, the shine of the moon, the warmth of the sun, the *nazm* of Faiz, the writings of Gulzar. He was my peace, an unattainable longing.

We seemed to be lost in the past, forgetting our present moments. It was the future we thought about and changed our past once. We had been together for more than five years, enough to know him in and out, enough to survive the trivialities that love offers. But perhaps our stars disagreed to align. We were brave, we didn't give up on each other but predestination or free will, who overrules? I got my answer. What had started with two different people who never believed in love coming too close, had ended with wounds so deep that they shivered at our beliefs of love again. Nothing happened, just days passed and with each growing day, we were shown reasons to prove that we are misfits. We had struggled and despite trying to save ourselves, we ruined it to be toxic. It was evident that it was the tomb of our love, and we were offering flowers to it. It would not bloom. Yet, Hope is a disguised salesman that convinces you to hold on. From dreaming of a home with him to planning the rest of our lives, we had gone too far to erase our last traces from each other's hearts.

I remember the last time we met to end our love; I was in tears. He went up that footbridge waving goodbye, turning around and looking at me as if it was for the last time. So many efforts and my destiny were conquered! Seeing him today on a random train to Chandigarh, sitting in the same first-class compartments meant again our fates intertwined as if he was meant to be in my life again.

'How have you been?' he asked.

I was too overwhelmed to say anything. I was in tears and in an attempt to hide my misery, with a brief pause I rushed into the washroom.

I didn't know why was this happening. Why did we meet again? It was hard to let him go previously. I was supposed to do this again and I didn't dare to stoop down again. I knew I would be broken this time.

His message swiped across my phone screen, 'We are in this together, remember. I am not even able to figure it out. Instead of you talking to yourself and doing the calculations, let's try to figure it out together.'

I came out and knocked at his door. He greeted me with a wide smile, 'I am so happy that I met you again.'

He tried to make me comfortable.

At this point, I didn't know anything about him for the past two years. All that was left between us was the formal exchange of birthday wishes. I didn't know if he was hitched or engaged or married and wondered if his falling into either category bothered me or not. He asked me about my reason to be on the train and he told me his. He had the rank he had always dreamt of, and I felt happy and proud of him. He then happened to ask if I still speak that incessantly, if I still get grumpy, if I am still scared of loud voices, if I still love mountains if I still behave like a kid. He had reframed his question instead of simply asking, 'If I was still the same person, I was two years ago.'

This made me nostalgic, or I don't know what, I just hugged him tightly. I could feel his tears near my ears. He tried to calm me down. I just wanted us not to break apart. I wanted time to stop and run that moment into a loop of infinity. I wanted to hug him tightly and never be apart. We had ended because things were unfavourable, we did it wishing for each other's happiness. It was a cold-blooded irony because I could figure out that our happiness was with each other and still we were traveling on different roads. I was crying while talking, I had no idea if he could comprehend my words mixed with deep breaths and a base voice and coughs all mixed. He asked me to calm down singing, *"Lag jaa gale ki fir yeh haseen shaam hon aa ho, shayad fir iss janam mein mulaakat hon aa naa..."* (Just hug, because this evening will never come again, maybe we will never meet in this birth.)

He was aware of the hidden old-school romantic in me, he knew my love for songs in his voice, and this time, he didn't spoil the moment by singing the Punjabi songs that I fail to interpret. His arrow was more accurate than ever. It went straight through my heart. I felt that solace. I could hear him placing an order over his phone to Comseum asking them to deliver a pizza at the next station. He remembered all this meant. I still had the chance of my name being against him. I hugged him tighter, and we lost ourselves in each other's eyes, talking and relishing the moment more than anything. He held my hand only to see that it was the same watch that he had given me. He showed me his wallet which bore my photograph. Everything seemed too perfect or rather too good to be true. Then came our pizza, and all he said was, 'Would you please share your pizza with me for the rest of your life?'

A blissful moment, right? This was what I had wanted. A perfect life!! My love is immortalized and tying a mortal knot with his soul.

And I woke up from this dream. All that I had was hope in all the hopelessness.

14

Implicit Heart

Chandni Ahuja

Strolling by the nearby park on a sunny day, Alex felt extremely joyful and calm. He was exhilarated to celebrate the young night with his gorgeous young beau, Gabriel. It was Gabriel's first birthday away from Alex as he had to move out of New York for over six months to study Psychology. Feeling proud and happier than ever, Alex wished him luck and bid him goodbye for a few months that felt like ages.

Gabriel and Alex had an extraordinary love story, just like any other love bird. Alex always procured immense joy and pride in calling Gabriel his boyfriend. On a strange stormy night, the two had crossed paths and did not even realize it. It seemed as if it were destiny for both to meet each other at that very right moment. Alex was a grown young man in his mid-twenties who had just started up a cosmetics company. It went all fine until one day when Alex was almost about to lose his temper, he bumped into Gabriel. Little did he know that the sly smirk which Gabriel showcased as a friendly customer, would turn out into something consistent, natural, and beautiful. Right from that day, the two peacefully continued their journey loving each other through all the good and bad times.

Gabriel was a soft-hearted person in his early twenties and was an empath. Alex had his heart broken many times, to be counted. Never in his wildest dreams did he imagine stepping outside into the romantic world, let alone his vulnerable guard down for anyone. But eventually, when Gabriel and Alex found their lingering hearts clinging onto each other, they continued their loving journey for almost two successful years and cherished every minute of their love.

At present, it had been over three weeks since Gabriel had left town, and all Alex could do was think of him. He could not get enough of Gabriel's lavender plum scent gushing his mind on lonely nights, and the noise ghosts of their banter around the kitchen counter of who was a better cook interrupting his nap. Alex kind of regretted not being able to meet him for such long months so he had a brief moment of thinking. He lay on the brown leather couch that he and Gabriel bought together from the local store, only to sit and contemplate all the possibilities of things going wrong if he surprised Gabriel. He suddenly hopped off his couch and picked up his laptop. He searched for tickets to Toronto. He was astonished to find a flight ticket straight to Toronto on Saturday night, exactly when it was Gabriel's birthday. Without giving it a second thought, Alex made the most out of his excitement. He quickly booked the flight tickets and made the required cab arrangements. Alex Skyped his lover and tried to keep his cool but could not help but smile the whole time. Gabriel was feeling invigorated after a bright yoga session with his classmates, and he talked about his day to Alex as he noticed something different and felt quite bewildered. Somehow, Alex convinced him that he was happy because he had just returned home with a box of Swiss chocolate waffles and donuts.

Alex got ready in his fresh suit and rushed to the airport. He told Gabriel that he was just going to visit his granny over the weekend, so Gabriel tried not to disturb him for some quality time with his granny. Gabriel was not much of a birthday party fan so he couldn't care any less about his own. After heading to the airport in Toronto,

Alex jumped out with joy. He waited for his cab while fooling his lover over the phone. He called Gabriel and told him that he should be ready to meet up with an experienced Psychologist, George, by the evening who was conducting an enlightening workshop for everyone. In the evening, Gabriel thought of it and headed to the given address. He was completely unaware of his lover's acquaintance with his classmates. Walking down the street, he received a call from his parents who surprised him by saying they were coming to meet him. Gabriel felt happy to meet them after so long and blurted out the information to Alex.

Alex was the one and only one who invited his parents over. Unlike Alex's open-minded parents, Gabriel's always maintained their image, prestige, and reputation in the town. His parents always tried to be the most loving and perfect family around to impress and please people around them. Just like they say, like father, like son, Gabriel had inherited the fear of society. He could not bear to think of what society may think of his character. Alex always thought that Gabriel was frank with his parents. Imagining that his parents knew about them, Alex had decided to settle. He deep down knew that Gabriel was the only one outside. He knew that regardless of how many fish were out there in the sea, Gabriel would be his soulmate. On his way to the town, Alex had stopped by the most expensive jewelry shop to buy a diamond ring for the proposal. After rummaging through huge boxes of rings, he finally settled on one, with a rose gold plate around the corner which was probably a brownie point for him. It all seemed like the cherry on the top as Alex headed to Gabriel's dorm with the most gorgeous and exquisite ring inside his pocket.

When Gabriel heard a familiar knock on the dusty wooden door, froze for a moment. His parents reached out to grasp the situation and found a man in a neat black coat suit standing outside with a pleasant bouquet of red flowers. His parents wondered what was so shocking for their son to gasp at the presence of a piece of chad in the flesh. Alex never realized his identity had been squeezed into nothing until Gabriel introduced him to his parents as his long-lost childhood friend from school. Alex was astonished to find how he belittled their love into nothingness. Just then, Gabriel's parents shook him off his thinking and invited him inside. Alex bluntly smiled and greeted them.

Alex kept staring at his lover across the room as everyone from the family sat down to have some dinner. He kept reminiscing about how he did not acknowledge that Gabriel's parents did not know about them. Gabriel had promised him and told him that he had already come out to his parents and that they accepted him as he was. Alex was encumbered and completely bothered by the lies he fed to his parents the moment he arrived and the way he had lied to his face.

Alex was all by himself on the lawn, staring at the scenery after dinner. He felt like going inside the room and getting to talk to Gabriel about it, but he could not. Gabriel was occupied with his dad at work so Alex tried not to disturb him further. Just a few minutes later, Gabriel's little sister came by running around the lawn to find Alex looking lost. She asked him if something was wrong, and he denied it to avoid any trouble. The little girl, Sasha knew that there were some lingering feelings that Alex was hiding so out of wonder, she asked him whether he liked and missed Gabriel. Hearing such a thing, Alex tried his best to give off vibes the other way around. He laughed it off and told her that it was all in her head and knelt to tell her how much his big brother loved him. Alex started telling her stupid stories of how Gabriel tried to cook food and failed, and how protective he was of his little girl.

Suddenly, Sasha hugged him and said, 'I know Gabriel means something to you... it's okay to be extra careful about your friends and love them,' and left him saying goodnight.

Alex had never realized that such a small girl could understand so many intense emotions and feelings. He had forgotten the actual purpose he had come to meet Gabriel for. He tried his best to not focus on the worst-case scenario and headed back to his bed for the night. Early in the morning, he was surprised to see Gabriel lying next to him. Gabriel apologized to him for not paying enough attention to him. He expressed his love for him and explained how afraid he was of losing his parents by scraping off the "perfect son" title. Alex understood his situation but could not help the piercing words slipping off his tongue. Alex made him realize how much effort he had put into traveling down to surprise him, by just hanging on to the loose strings of Gabriel telling him that his parents knew the truth.

Alex stood up and said, 'I loved you, and I still do. So much that you never realized my worth at all. All you had to do was trust yourself. You had to have some faith in the bond we had and in me. Every time you had the chance, you denied the truth and showed your parents a face that was never you. I thought you were different and something else. I saw you and loved you for someone who would go to all extents just like I did, every time you needed assurance. But all of this dog and pony show only describes how little you think of our love. It makes me think otherwise. I had come down here to make you mine, to express all that my heart desires in you, but it seems like I was utterly wrong about it. It only makes me rethink every stupid decision I ever made in my life that I now regret.'

Gabriel gazed at Alex and his unsaid feelings with teary eyes. Alex stared right at Gabriel with a pitiful face as he realized that even though Gabriel loved him a lot more than he did himself, he would never in his dreams try to shatter himself off from the little bubble. Alex understood Gabriel's silence to be the end of what they had continued for years.

As Gabriel moved closer, Alex held his hands and said, 'I know you are strong, and you will achieve everything one day. Maybe, this was not just the right time for the two of us. I have understood that you love me, but I hope one day you find someone as loving as you are, and break off your shell and prove the world wrong by taking pride in showing who you truly are.' Gabriel whispered in his ears how badly he wanted to have all of him for his entire life, but he deeply regretted not trying. Alex paused, pulled Gabriel by his neck, and kissed him a long goodbye. Gabriel shed tears while kissing him back and gripping his hair tight around his long fingers. It was the one last kiss they were meant to have, and they made the most of it. Alex stared right into Gabriel's eyes and held his face, caressing his soft fingers around his beautiful eyes, and plump lips for the last time as he kissed his forehead and wished him luck. He turned back to pack his bags and just then, Gabriel grabbed his hands and requested him to visit the beach for one time with him in silence.

The two of them drove in the car playing their favorite album by The Beatles and smiled at each other. When they reached the beach, Gabriel and Alex sat down barefoot, gazing at the slight movements of the salty waves. In those brief silences at the beach, where two kids wandered around running behind their parents, the two wandering souls seeking love and acceptance watched their faith slowly stripping away. It seemed as if the waves came by and crushed off the lucid images of Alex deep-rooted inside his head, of building a life with his soulmate as Gabriel sat in disguise, wanting to just take one step at a time and do better in life.

15

Their Sad Destiny

Naina Khemani

'We will meet again in our next lives,' said Liam.

Ina and Liam were both on the verge of death due to a mishap that took place while they were driving to their honeymoon spot. Bit by bit, life force was draining from their eyes as they held each other close even though the strength left their bodies. Suddenly there was a pin-drop silence around them. It felt like time had frozen and Liam could hear his heartbeat rising, as his wounds seemed to be healing at a visible speed.

Ignoring this strange phenomenon, all of his attention was on his loved one, Ina. Seeing Ina slowly close her eyes, he gets very scared and despite his injuries and pain, he frantically shook her and said, 'Ina, Ina… Please wake up. I will not be able to live without you. Please! I love you, Ina, please don't leave me. Please, I beg you, okay? Please!'

He seemed hysterical and repeatedly said the same thing.

Looking at his beloved's cold body in his arms, he seemed to have received a huge shock and just sat there staring at her blankly, as teardrops mixed with blood fell down his eyes. He didn't even comprehend that he was sitting there all safe and fine without a single scratch on his body, his injuries seemed to have vanished into thin air.

Suddenly, various images and memories started appearing in his mind. The memories pierced his head like a thousand needles, as he clutched his head and bent down screaming with agonizing pain.

The pain was so agonizing enough that he fell unconscious shortly after. When Liam opened his eyes, all he saw was darkness. He could not comprehend where he was and also didn't seem to remember the accident. He just stared blankly at the void. Suddenly, he saw a ray of light coming from far away and it was compelling him to walk toward it, so he did just that. As he approached closer, the light got brighter, and he had to shield his eyes from the blinding light. He stepped into the light with closed eyes and when he opened them, he seemed to have stepped into a whole new world. There were people all around him with strange clothing and they were going about their business. No one seemed to notice him.

As he slowly started walking, he accidentally bumped into a lady and was about to apologize when the lady said, 'Ahh, how could I bump into nothing? Is the witch here again?' and started looking around her frantically. Seeing no abnormalities, she heaved a sigh of relief and dusted her hand on her clothes, while walking further. Seeing this, Liam gets shocked that no one can see him, and also about the fact that the lady spoke in a strange language, but he was able to comprehend it.

He was sure that he hadn't heard such a language his whole life. As he started walking further wondering about the 'witch' the lady was muttering about, he suddenly got a strange feeling that he couldn't put into words.

Just like that, he had been wandering and looking around this strange place for a whole day taking advantage of the fact that he was invisible. He kept inspecting everything and was amazed by the strange things in that place. Now, after a whole day of wandering around, he felt extremely tired.

'How did I get here? Just where is this place?' he thought out loud to himself.

He then started to explore more and wondered, 'I am forgetting something very important, but what?'

Just as this thought crossed his mind, he suddenly felt a piercing pain in his head and unable to withstand it, he fell unconscious. When he regained consciousness, he found out that he was lying on a bed. While slowly sitting up, he started inspecting his surroundings.

'Where am I?' he asked himself.

He then looked around and realized that he was in a room of a cottage-like shelter. At that moment, the door to the room opened, and in walked a very beautiful woman. She was beautiful just like an enchantress, with healthy pale white skin, phoenix-like eyes, plump lips, and wavy and silky dark brown hair that went up to her feet. It would not be too much to say that she was an embodiment of the goddess herself. But strangely, looking at the woman, Liam felt nothing but a strong resentment and hatred. He was shocked that he felt such strong negative emotions toward a woman he had never met before.

The woman walked towards him with a smiling face and sat on the bed beside him. She leaned forward and traced her fingers upon his face, starting from his eyes, nose, jaw, and finally to his lips. She just sat there strangely staring at him. Liam felt very uncomfortable with all this skinship and the way she stared at him. He was also confused by the emotions of hatred and resentment he felt toward this unfamiliar woman.

Waking up from his stupor, he got shocked and blurts out, 'Wait! You can see me?'

The woman just laughed and replied, 'Of course, I can see you. I have always been watching you.'

Listening to this, he got the weird feeling again in his guts.

He asked, 'Who are you? Where is this place? And why am I here?'

She replied, 'This is the place you rightfully belong to. Here, with me. I am your lover.'

'But I am not from here and I have to go and be with my… With my… Who should I be with?' as he said, he felt that piercing pain again and clutched his head in extreme agony.

The woman came over and wandered her hand on his head and Liam could feel the pain slowly subsiding.

'Just who are you? And why am I here?' he asked again.

'Take rest. You will know everything very soon,' she said ambiguously and walked away.

Feeling exhausted, he chose to lie down and started thinking about things that had happened until then. While thinking, he wandered his gaze around the room and noticed a strange, but familiar carving on the only table in the room. He willed his body to get up and went near the table to inspect the carving and confirm his suspicion. Indeed, the carving looked exactly similar to the tattoo that he had on his body. He got that uneasy feeling again. After looking more closely, he found that the only difference between the tattoo and the carving was that the carving had an additional word engraved on it, which was '*Remember*'.

The weird feeling got stronger, and he felt that he was forgetting something very important. He started looking through the room for other clues that could answer all his questions and quell that weird feeling he had. Unfortunately, after searching through the whole room, he didn't find anything useful. Just as he was about to lie down again, he accidentally slipped down and noticed a piece of paper sticking out from the folds of the bed which he missed earlier while searching through the room. Taking out the note, he opened it and read the content written in it.

It read, "*Ina... Witch... You must remember... Go to your world... Save her.... Ina... Run... Don't miss the...chance again...run Ina.*"

The writing was a bit messy and unrecognizable like it was written in a hurry. It took him a lot of effort to make out the words, but when he did, suddenly, all the memories came back to him.

He got very flustered and started running towards the door when suddenly more and more memories started appearing in his head, and he just froze. In the memory, he saw himself and Ina living many lives as lovers, but it would always end tragically just as they get married in each life. The memory stopped at the scene of the accident, where he was holding Ina in his arms.

He felt various emotions of anger, sadness, regret, pain, and resentment rushing through him. It was too much for him to handle. As he ran out of the door, he came face to face with that beautiful woman.

Seeing her, he shouted, 'Just who in the world are you?! Please let me go back to my Ina. Please! I beg you, please send me back!'

The woman walked closer to him with the same sickening smile, 'I see you have regained your memories, huh? (tsk). It's better this way. It would be more fun to see you powerless and in agony,' she said.

'What do you mean?' Liam asked.

'What do I mean?' She repeated after him, 'Hmm... What do I mean? Didn't you see me in your memories? Aww... I am very hurt that you didn't remember me, you know?' She continued in a mocking tone.

Liam then remembered that this woman was also present in the first lives of him and Ina. She also fell in love with him in that life, but he only had eyes for his Ina. In reality, that beautiful woman is a witch who everybody feared. She was called Aurora and was a very ruthless witch. Aurora confessed her feelings to Liam, but he rejected her and even said that he was disgusted with her and her immoral acts, which angered Aurora.

'I curse you! You both will never be able to live a fulfilling life with each other. Just as you get the happiness of getting married, the next moment, it will be taken away from you. Your happiness will be short-lived and turn into immense sorrow, as your lover will be bestowed with the most painful death. And you Liam, you will have to live the rest of your life without your beloved, in every incarnation. And you both will keep repeating this cycle, again and again in every reincarnation. And just as your life comes to an end, you will travel back to this world, to live with me, never able to go back to your world in that life again. You will live in unknown pain of missing something for the rest of your life in that reincarnation, slowly falling in love with me and not regaining your memories until your death, because you will have no choice,' she ruthlessly put a curse on him.

The carving and note were left there by one of his reincarnations to make his other reincarnations remember everything.

As he remembered everything, he collapsed and started crying while shouting at the top of his lungs.

'Why, why did you do this to me… To us? I never loved you! I only love my Ina… Give her back to me you witch!' He lunged at her while shouting this, but with a wave of her hand, Aurora stopped him and plunged a knife straight through his heart and watched as he slowly died.

'Tsk tsk tsk… How did he regain his memories so soon in this life? It shouldn't have happened until he was on the verge of death. Looks like I have to do some reinforcements to prepare for his next arrival,' she said devilishly and walked away without turning back.

And then, this cycle went on till eternity, but Liam and Ina never united because of one sinister heart.

16

The Knee Proposal Part I

Rohan P. Lapalikar

Shlok is a simple guy who works in the IT sector, apparently, quite satisfied with his work life. He lives with his parents and a younger brother who is about to graduate. He has a condition, in medical terms, called Allergic rhinitis. Some nasal nerves in his nose are sensitive to dust, smoke, and pollution; sometimes it gets triggered due to weather changes. As advised, he always carries a nasal spray, which gives him temporary relief from allergies and constant sneezing. His two friends, Megha and Sumeet, whom he trusts more than himself, stood by his side always, till date. Long ago, there was a time in their school days, when this trio was exceptionally famous, with Sumeet as a third wheel. So, here's the love triangle, Sumeet loved Megha, Megha loved Shlok, but Shlok was flirty. There was not one girl in their class to whom he hadn't proposed. Megha was, then, the most beautiful girl in their class. But Shlok had an ideology of enjoying every moment of life with a variety of people. AHH! The good old days.

***

Present, July 2021

It was Shlok's birthday, so he took a half-day from his office after Megha and Sumeet insisted on a small get-together at his place. In a black formal shirt and grey trousers, he stood outside the building waiting for a taxi. He checked his watch just to realize he was on time. Ten minutes later, the weather turned slightly. It started to rain and quickly, he and other people nearby rushed to take some shelter under the bus stop hood which was a stone-throw distance from the building. This sudden rain and dust in the air triggered his allergy and he started sneezing. So, he opened up his bag to take the nasal spray, which was in the inner compartment. But there were two nasal sprays, one functional and another one, around 4 years old and now empty. With a black permanent marker, "*09/09/2018*", in shabby scribbly handwriting, was written on a masking tape stuck to the spray nozzle. Mistakenly, he took the latter one out instead of the functional spray nozzle. He glanced at it for a few moments as some nostalgia ran through his memories. He kept it back, took the new spray, and inhaled it via both nostrils. As he sprayed, a painful memory resurfaced.

***

5 years ago, Sept 2016

Sipping some hot water with turmeric, and an inhaler on the other hand, Shlok stood facing towards the window looking at dark clouds outside.

'Why? Because I am not good enough?' he asked Nisha, his then-girlfriend. He shivered as he grew more and more despondent.

'No. It has nothing to do with you. It is all on me, right?' Nisha asked in sarcasm.

'Stop! You know, just stop this, blame-game thing. You did not think about it even once? Not only that, but you know just once, how will Shlok feel after I confess?' he asked.

With frequent pauses and low tones, Nisha tried to end their conversation, 'Yes. Blame-game thing, wow! You know, Tanay never blames me if I blame him for anything.'

'Then he is dumb, an ass, he is not your boyfriend he is just…' he panicked and stopped, thinking that he is hurting Nisha.

'Toy? Fling? Go ahead, don't stop. He is just. What?' Nisha questioned him in a rude tone.

'He is just a stupid dumb-ass kid who thinks it is okay, to have an arrogant, stubborn girlfriend. Like you!' Shlok took a brief pause, 'He will regret it, and you will leave him one day. The same way it's happening now. Mark my words Nisha, and trust me,' he wiped his tears and gathered courage, 'trust me if it was me at your place, I would never have done this to you.'

'Okay. Good for you. I will mark your words. Don't worry, I will manage,' Nisha replied.

Shlok was hurt and disappointed. For him, things just turned upside down in a matter of a couple of weeks. From failing in a happy relationship to failing in his 1st semester, from a third-wheel intervention to losing the girl he loved, from losing a best friend to losing many friends, all of it broke him. But Shlok was bold and strong-willed when it came to his morals and ethics. He refused to use another girl as a source to move on from Nisha, even if it was the last option. In due course, he fell sick. He couldn't bear all this. With his appetite lost, he couldn't concentrate on his studies and his home as well. As advised by doctors, he spent most of the time sleeping and thinking about Nisha's betrayal. His mom called Sumeet, who was now a doctor, and told him about Shlok's health and unhappy mood. Sumeet, being his best friend since his school days, immediately visited him along with Megha.

'Oh God, what just happened to you? Didn't we have a conversation a week back, where you said it's all fine?' Megha asked with concern as they both sat near him. Shlok replied with a pause of a few seconds. Now that Sumeet and Megha were in his room, Sumeet closed the door, so they could talk in privacy.

'Hey, man. Speak up! Is it because of Nisha? We both are all ears, make it fast. I might get a call from the hospital any time soon,' Sumeet said.

'No Sumeet wait, it's something unusual,' Megha said as she tried to read Shlok's face. She picked up Shlok's phone to read Nisha's WhatsApp messages and unlocked it using her fingerprint.

'May I, if you don't mind?' she asked. To which, Shlok nodded to say yes.

Sumeet and Megha read his WhatsApp conversation with Nisha.

'Oh. Say what? Let me get this straight,' she glanced at Sumeet, 'she was in a relationship with you. She roamed with you for, like, 3 years or so. And then realized, Tanay is better. Who the hell is this Tanay, some college guy?' Megha questioned in anger.

'Yea,' Shlok replied in a low voice.

'Dude! It's okay, you need to relax, man. You took your medicine?' Sumeet asked.

'I cannot. Relax!' Shlok smiled and exclaimed, 'I am disturbed. I am broke, and right now, perhaps beyond repair. So please!'

Sumeet's phone rang a few seconds later, 'God no!' he exclaimed.

'You had food? And medicines?' Megha held Shlok's hand and asked.

'Guys, I think I have to go back to the clinic. Megha, you stay here and take care of him, I will be back,' Sumeet hung up the call and said to Megha.

As he was leaving, Shlok stopped him and hugged him. 'Thanks a lot, buddy. Thanks for checking up on me,' he said.

'Shut the front door, you idiot!' Sumeet said to Shlok, 'And don't die. She ain't worth your life.'

After Sumeet left, Megha helped him organize his worktable, which was too untidy to see. 'Should I make some coffee for us?' she asked.

'No, no coffee for me, you have it. I'll have green tea,' Shlok replied to Megha as he desperately waited for Nisha's message and checked his phone.

While Megha made tea and coffee, she had a polite and very friendly conversation with Shlok's mom. She was the only one in his friend circle who considered Shlok's family as her own. Shlok's family considered Megha a good company for Shlok to be with. But the questions from his mom were quite difficult to be answered, for his family was too traditional. Megha blamed it on college food and study pressure. Also, it's manageable, she added.

When she returned, Shlok was facing his window and checking his inbox to see if Nisha messaged. Megha offered him his cup of green tea.

'Thanks,' he said as he kept his phone aside and grabbed the cup.

'Keep checking, as if she will ever message,' Megha giggled, 'Better concentrate on your green tea because, unlike Nisha, this is good for your health.'

'What? Will you, please,' Shlok got irritated and disturbed, 'stop. Just stop throwing tantrums. It's bothering me.'

'Yes of course Shlok, it should bother you. It's all because of you,' Megha replied hastily.

'Yes, go ahead. I have already played this blame game before,' Shlok said to her, showing her index and middle finger, 'Twice!'

'Yes, both of them are on you,' Megha kept her coffee mug aside, 'You know, think about it. A few years back, I approached you.'

'That time I wasn't...' Shlok interrupted, but Megha didn't let him.

'I knew, you are flirty. I knew you wouldn't be a keeper. I knew you would leave me. But I was ready to face it. Face it all. Ready to get hurt. All I wanted was one chance. One fucking chance, Shlok, to give you the love you always deserved.'

Megha took a brief pause and, realizing Shlok is traumatized, tried to control her anger, 'Look. The world does not function as we want. It functions as it is made, full of questions,' she stated and held his hand, to show that she still cares as before. Shlok turned towards her and made eye contact, 'We just have to find someone, who is ready to find answers with us.'

'Megha, I know I messed up. Okay? And I do realize, this Nisha wouldn't have ruined me if she was not my girlfriend,' he said.

'But, here's the thing. What Nisha did the day before yesterday, is not as traumatizing as the thought of taking you for granted if you were my girlfriend,' he added.

Megha made eye contact, 'Whatever we have between us, is more beautiful, more divine than any other possibility of what could have been. Let's assume you were my girlfriend, and we broke up for some reason,'

Megha laughed and teased him to make the moment light, 'How unlucky!'

'I know. And who would have made me this green tea,' he said and pointed to his cup, 'without honey, idiot!'

Megha was still holding his hand and realized she forgot to add any sweetener, 'What?' she asked shockingly.

Both of them giggled and Shlok nodded. With their hands still entangled, Shlok glanced at their intertwined fingers and wished if that moment could temporarily freeze. With a brief silence between both of them, Shlok slowly pulled her close and grabbed her coffee mug to keep aside. Slowly he touched the space between her cheeks and hair and gave her a serene look. Shlok came forward with closed eyes, and a peaceful grip of their hands softly kissed her forehead. A moment later, Megha opened her eyes and so did Shlok. She rested her head on his shoulder amid a hug.

'Megha,' Shlok called her name as he caressed her hair.

'Hmm?' she asked in a peaceful low tone.

'Thank you,' he said.

'For this green tea in which I forgot to add honey?' she asked.

'No. Thank you for just existing. I am glad,' he replied.

Megha smiled and hugged him even tighter with an assurance that she would always be there for him.

***

As months passed by, Shlok was struggling to forget Nisha. In April 2017, he appeared for his 1st semester backlog exam, and he made it this time. Things started to slowly come on track, but some wounds were still open. Sumeet shifted to Bangalore, his hometown. Megha started working in a corporate firm and her office was adjacent to Shlok's. Megha often used to call him and meet on random occasions, so she could distract him from some disturbing thoughts. Both were unaware of what was coming!

***

June 2017

Wearing a maroon shirt and jeans, Shlok stood in front of the mirror making cuffs from his sleeves when his mom entered.

'Wow. Anything special that I missed?' she asked in astonishment.

'Yes. It's Megha's birthday you forgot. She invited me, and some other friends for dinner,' he replied as he sprayed a puff of deodorant on his shirt. He turned back and beside him, in a paper bag was a parcel which he handed over to her, 'Just have a look at what I am gifting her.'

His mom opened up the box, and inside there was a photo frame with the polaroid photo of him and Megha that was the first photo from his new camera. But the photo was framed UPSIDE DOWN which confused his mom. Along with that a short letter,

Thank you, for turning my life upside down. Please don't forget you are a part of me, and you will always be. Congratulations on turning 22.

With love and care,

Your favorite P.I.T.A

'PITA? What is that?' his mom asked.

'Pain In the Ass,' he whispered, and she laughed.

'Bye. I will be home by 10, her dad will drop me off,' he said while he opened the main door of their house.

'Shlok, listen,' said his mom and he turned back.

'Yes darling?' he asked.

'You look happy. I missed you this way,' she complimented.

'Thank you. I love you, Mom,' he said and left after she replied, 'I love you too!'

Shlok left.

17

The Knee Proposal Part II

Rohan P. Lapalikar

Megha was that one person in his social circle, who made him forget all his problems in an instant. Unfortunately, Shlok never felt the same for her. Right at her home, Megha opened the door and greeted Shlok with excitement and a hug.

She held his hand and pulled him into the house, 'Come in babe!' she said.

'Where's the food?' he asked.

'First, just come in and relax, enjoy the party, lighten your mood, or do you have to just hop on the food?' she asked.

Megha had invited five more friends. Out of them, there was a girl named Vrunda, her cousin. With just a glance at her, while exploring the guests, Shlok lost his senses.

Megha offered him a bottle of soft drink, 'Come here, I'll introduce you to them,' she said.

'Guys! This is Shlok,' she said to her other friends and held his arms, 'My Soulmate-friend.'

A quick meet and greet happened between all of them and he introduced himself to Vrunda. Shlok started to develop feelings for her and called Megha onto the balcony.

'Listen. That girl in a purple t-shirt, Vrunda, how is she?' Shlok asked Megha on her balcony.

'Seriously Shlok? Vrunda?' she shockingly asked, 'She is not your type.'

'What is this type and all? Just call her here, and let's talk. Just you, me, and her,' he said.

Megha was continuously hesitating since she was her sister. But Shlok seemed adamant, Megha was not sure. The Shlok she has seen in her past was not a one-woman guy, which Vrunda deserved. Shlok had a disturbing history with his first serious girlfriend, and the same with Nisha, the second one. This pain of unreciprocated love for Shlok, Megha had already felt.

'Shlok I understand she is attractive, but she is my sister, and I cannot let her be the victim of your uncertainty,' she expressed her concern to Shlok.

'Megha, nothing like that would happen. Trust me! I am not Nisha,' Shlok said and Megha called Vrunda on the balcony. But just a few seconds later, Vrunda got a call from her home, and she had to rush back. While going, she hugged Megha and her mom and left. Unfortunately, Shlok couldn't talk to her that day. The very same night, Shlok didn't sleep as he was continuously thinking about Vrunda. He followed her on Instagram and the next day, she followed him back. They started talking and it sparked with Vrunda too. Both had their insecurities playing a part in maintaining distance from the other one. Vrunda was insecure about Shlok turning out to be like her ex. Shlok was insecure because he did not want to break her heart. Both of them went ahead with what their heart said.

***

After a few months, Shlok finally approached Vrunda to meet in person.

'Hey! Do you like hot chocolate?' he asked.

'Of course. Why so? Are you asking me out?' she replied.

'What? No. Why would I ask you out? We are not in a relationship, so!' he said.

'Yea. I was thinking the same thing, like why would you ask me out,' she said with sarcasm.

'Yes, I was asking you out. So tomorrow Nerul station? 6 pm?' he finally said.

'Done. 5:30 pm. See you at Nerul station,' she said.

The next day at the decided time, Shlok stood at the ticket counter with a rose, he was nervous. From the lobby of the station, he spotted Vrunda coming towards him in the same purple T-shirt that she wore when they first met, and his eyesight was stuck on her.

'Surprise! You remember this t-shirt?' she asked after they subtly hugged.

Shlok paused with shyness, 'Yes, I do,' he said and offered his hand for her to hold, and she accepted. As she held his hand, Shlok felt heavenly.

This was the vibe that Shlok had missed in all his temporary relationships, and Vrunda never stood a chance in her past relationships. During those moments they spent together, Vrunda opened up and Shlok didn't get bored, and vice versa. Vrunda was charming.

'You are good. I like your nature,' Vrunda said as they were having a cup of hot chocolate, 'Can I ask you something?'

He blushed, 'Sure! Go ahead.'

'You smile with pain or are you always smiling?' she asked as she could sense something unusual in his smile.

He took a pause. Now that he was strong enough to handle the trauma of his 1st girlfriend and Nisha's behavior, he said with a gentle smile, 'I am always smiling. It's just that, my face is a God gift.'

Vrunda nodded with a giggle, 'Okay. That's a good reply.'

Later that night, it was half past 11 when Shlok's phone vibrated. He checked and it was a text message from Vrunda stating, "Next time don't hesitate to tell the truth, I won't judge."

"So, when is the next time?" he replied.

"I will go to Meghna's home on the weekend, her parents will be out. Why don't you join us and stay for a day?" she asked, and Shlok agreed immediately.

"Sure thing. See you this weekend," he replied.

***

Shlok knocked on the door, and Megha opened it in household clothes.

'Are you serious right now?' she shouted out of surprise and hugged him. He offered a bottle of soft drink.

'Surprise baby!' Vrunda said she munched a slice of pizza.

Shlok removed his backpack and kept it on the side table in her hall. He gently hugged Vrunda and she curled her hands around him.

'Stay along. My parents aren't there till tomorrow afternoon.' Megha said.

Hesitating, Shlok looked at Vrunda and she gave a weird smile, 'Please! Muaaahh!'

'Okay!' Shlok replied awkwardly, 'I already bought my clothes lmao.'

'P.I.T.A. like always.' Megha sighed. Shlok winked at Vrunda.

That day when Shlok wanted to open his heart out to Megha, but not knowing Vrunda properly is what stopped him. They were all tired after eating and watching Harry Potter and decided to sleep. Vrunda went to the bedroom, and Shlok and Megha sat on the couch. After some time, Megha leaned on his shoulder and held his hands.

'Are you okay?' he asked.

'Yes. You aren't. What's bothering you Shlok?' she asked.

After a pause, 'Megha next month I will have to go for an internship in Ahmedabad. I won't be here for over a month.'

As he said, Megha wrapped themselves in a blanket, 'I don't know how am I going to spend a month without seeing you both. What about Aai & Baba? I am concerned,' he expressed.

'Guys, I am not able to sleep. Can I join you?' Vrunda came out and spoke.

'It will be okay. Don't worry,' Megha said to Shlok and asked Vrunda to sit on the couch.

Megha went inside. Now Shlok and Vrunda had some time alone to talk.

'I was just 5 when Mom left me and Dad. I was just miserable for her,' resting her head on Shlok's lap she started speaking, 'Sometimes I think, I am not the product of love, but a compromise. Dad loved her from college days, but Mom didn't. Mom's parents wanted her to have an arranged marriage, but she was rejected. So, my dad approached, and she agreed on a few conditions. One of them was,'

Shlok interrupted and comforted her, 'Vrunda whatever happens, our financial conditions will not change my feelings. Okay!' he said.

'Shlok, I was in a relationship a few years back. His name was Aaryan. He was the mistake that,' she started shivering, 'I can never atone. He said only two things can lead to a happy life, Money, and Sex. (*She paused*) And I had no money to offer. He took everything for granted. Me, my dad, my money, my body, everything,' she started crying.

Shlok comforted her more, 'Hey! Stop...' he softly said. 'It's okay. The past is gone. Let it go.'

'Shlok I am afraid to commit. I have nothing to offer you, no job, no security. All I have is this life and I want to spend it with someone who loves me, someone who can go on his knees and propose to me, someone who is proud of me. Tell me how do I commit to you?' she asked to make eye contact with Shlok.

Shlok wiped her tears and dragged the blanket on her, 'Sleep. You are safe here.'

He started slowly brushing her hair and she fell asleep.

'Till death do us part!' he whispered to himself.

***

September 2018

While going to Ahmedabad, he waited for them at the station with his luggage and they arrived. Megha hugged him and so did Vrunda, he got emotional and sad.

Megha made him count his luggage with a checklist, which also included his nasal spray.

'I think I misplaced it,' he said shockingly.

'Wow! Idiot,' Megha said.

'Is it this one?' Vrunda asked as she too used the same nasal spray.

'Yes,' he said.

'Take it,' Vrunda handed it to him.

'But if I take this, what will you do?' Shlok asked.

'I'll purchase. Don't worry,' she said.

'I knew this would happen. I knew I was supposed to go, but I wasn't ready,' he said after keeping her nasal spray in the bag.

'Okay now, come on. The train will leave in a minute. Go keep your luggage and stay inside,' Megha said.

'Okay, I still have one minute left, right?' he asked them and gathered all the courage in him.

'Vrunda, listen to me carefully,' holding her arms he pulled her closer, 'When I come back, I will bow down on my knees and propose to you. I will talk to our parents about our marriage. I don't want anything. Let go of the past. Just you, me, and our future. A new start in a new world. And yes, I am proud to have you. Will you wait?' he asked in an affirmative manner making firm eye contact.

Vrunda gathered all her feelings and hugged him. In a sweet voice, she said, 'Yes. Yes, I will. Come back soon.'

Seeing all this Megha felt relieved as finally, Vrunda was loved after a very dark past. Shlok boarded the train and left.

***

This internship had a price. It took away the time that Shlok could give to Vrunda. Texts decreased. Calls reduced. Life got busy. He had a photo of Vrunda which he often kissed when he missed her. He got desperate to meet them. A week before the internship ended, Megha and Vrunda started ignoring his calls. Vrunda's last scene was stuck, and messages were undelivered. He managed his work in the last week and the next day early morning rushed back to Mumbai on a flight. He decided Megha would be the first person he would meet, but she didn't pick up his call several times. But neither did Vrunda. Around mid-morning, Shlok went to meet Vrunda with a rose and was anxious as to why she wasn't able to talk.

But this time, destiny had some other plans. To his shock, it was Vrunda's funeral. He saw her father, coming back from the cemetery after performing the last rituals. Her relatives were giving condolences and nowhere, her mom was to be seen. Shlok was devastated with disbelief.

Somewhere in the crowd, stood Megha, who approached Shlok outside the bungalow, and gave him a letter that Vrunda wrote.

Shlok, I am counting my days. By the time you read this, I might have reached the other side of the river. My liver cancer has gotten severe in the last few weeks. Megha didn't know about it. I don't have enough time. Please know, you were the last love of my life. Acceptance with unconditional love was my last wish, that you fulfilled. I am not dying unhappy. I am glad I met you. I am glad I found the one who was proud of me, someone who appreciates me. Once the nasal spray expires, don't use it, throw it away.

Till death DID us part.

With love.

Vrunda

It was traumatizing.

***

Present

His phone rang and he became conscious with teary eyes. A teardrop fell on Vrunda's nasal spray that he preserved after her death. He kept it in his pocket and used his nasal spray.

"Yes, Mom?" he asked on the phone.

"Okay. I will come by bus then," he said.

He boarded the next bus and reached home. Megha and his parents were waiting for him with a cake. He hugged them and said, 'Sorry to keep you waiting.'

In his room, which was messy, he kept his watch, wallet, and ID card on the table, along with that nasal spray, which Megha noticed. Shlok went inside the bathroom and Megha, who was curious, went to his room just to see that the nasal spray was her sister's. She got emotional as she was her only sister that was close to her, and she missed her every day, just like Shlok. Nostalgia ran through her mind as well. Shlok came out and saw Megha holding the nasal spray and her eyes were wet. They made eye contact with depressed smiles and Megha realized that she was wrong about Shlok and that he loved Vrunda with every inch of his feelings.

18

Love at the Sea-Shore

Ishat Sharma

This begins in Dehradun, the city of love, a story of an aristocratic family and a woman. There's no doubt because Dehradun is an academic and research hub. Home to millions. Several known institutes like the Indian Military Academy, Forest Research Institute, Indira Gandhi National Forest Academy, The Doon School, Welham Boys School, Welham Girls School, Rashtriya Indian Military College, Uttarakhand Ayurveda University, Wadia Institute of Himalayan Geology are here, but this city is also known for the Kapoor's, Aditya and Meera.

Everyone in the city desired to live the life that the Kapoors lived. Every woman in the city wished to have a charming man like Aditya Kapoor. He was handsome and had maintained his physique even in his 50s. Everyone in the city said, 'He is the epitome of the perfect husband, father, son, and what not.' He was a business tycoon and the only son of his parents, who lost their lives in a mishap when he was just 5. He spent most of the time in his office. He was devoted to his work. In the evening he came back home to spend time with his children. He had two sons and a daughter.

His wife, Meera, ran an NGO. She was a revolutionary who fought for women's fundamental rights, child labor, child marriage, etc. Fire and passion for social work were evident inside her. She was indeed an example of beauty with a brain. Her style, aura, way of speaking, and dressing sense everything was just perfect. Both of them had respect for each other. They had everything between them, except for the thing that made them complete–Love.

Everything appeared to be perfect, but only Kapoors knew the truth. It had been twenty years since their marriage, but they could never love each other completely. To sum up, their relationship was a compromise. Every time they had dinner together, solitude was felt.

Aditya was a good poet too, he had written many poems on love, but his inspiration was never Meera but a woman he had never met. Many times, Aditya had to go out for work. One fine evening he was getting ready for some business meetings in Goa where he had to stay for a week. At the dining table, he told his kids and wife that he was going out for a while and the kids asked him to bring something for them, but Meera just said, 'See you soon, Aditya.' It's very hard to live in a place where you have every worldly pleasure, everything you can buy, but the love of your companion, for them was a cage.

The next morning he reached Goa, checked into his hotel, and started preparing for his presentation. Everything went well concluding a deal that could change the level of his business. On the same day, he went to the beach and sat there with his laptop while watching the sunset. After some time, Aditya noticed a beautiful woman in the middle of the sea, laughing, enjoying the sunset, and playing with the water. Falling rays of the sun and shine from the water added up to her beauty and her smile felt like a miracle of nature. In her smile, Aditya saw how little of the world he had known. After a while, she came out of the sea and sat there with her eyes closed, looking above at the sky.

'Hello, I'm Aditya. Nice to see you,' Aditya said.

'Hey, Sara this side,' she replied, 'A 40-year-old with great ambitions, full of life and adventures...'

They started talking, and Sara told him about herself. She was an author who loved to write about life.

'I get happy seeing the wonders of nature, I believe in living the moment rather than wasting it,' she said. 'So, I have told enough about myself now it's your turn, Mr. Handsome, tell me about yourself,' she insisted.

'By profession, I'm a businessman from Dehradun. I'm married and blessed with three kids. Everyone in my family is busy in their own lives,' he said.

'What!' she exclaimed, 'You don't look like a married guy... Hahaha! You hardly look, 35?'

Both of them laughed heavily. They talked a lot, lost in each other that they forgot the time. After a while, Aditya invited her the next day for dinner at his place, and she couldn't deny it, they said Adios. There was something in her eyes, something strange Aditya noticed it but couldn't understand. It was like she wanted to say something, but she didn't.

The very next evening, she arrived at his place and knocked on the door. Aditya opened the door and kept looking at her. She looked like a queen in her outfit. Her simplicity took his heart away. The confidence, the spark in her eyes, her smile that seems like it can take all the loneliness of his.

Sara, on the other hand, commented to Aditya, 'Can't take my eyes off from a handsome man like you... ha-ha!'

'Says the very prettiest woman, maybe I'm looking handsome,' he replied.

'Please come in,' he said.

'Yes sure,' she replied.

She sat in the living room opposite each Aditya. Sara told Aditya

'Can I call you Adi, if you don't mind?'

'No worries, Madam,' he said. Aditya gave her a glass of wine, and they spent some quality time together. It appeared that Sara and Adi were lost in each other. Aditya was never such happy before. Sara started to like him, and Aditya liked her since he saw her but never told her.

When Sara was leaving, Aditya gave her the rose and said, 'It was nice meeting you, Sara,' and Sara left.

Sara kept smiling at him from inside the car until she left. Aditya and Sara kept on meeting each other for the sunset at the beach. They exchanged the digits. They became friends and eventually, more than friends.

One fine evening she asked him, 'Why do you look so lonely from the inside? You only smile for the unknown world. Why?'

He was silent for some time and then said, 'I show a fake smile to the world but after meeting you, I've learned to laugh and smile.'

Sara had a massive respect for him, she knew she loved him but hadn't the courage to say it. That night Aditya had drunk a lot and the next day was his flight to return to Dehradun. Sara stayed with him till morning on the beach. Aditya told her that he isn't happy with his wife, he lives in a relationship of settlement. He had never felt this before.

At this, Sara held his hand at the beach at midnight and said, 'You touched my soul at the horizon, and I could feel an eternity of never-ending love at your fingertips. The quest for love in my life is over.'

'I love you, Sara!' Aditya said.

'I love you too, Adi!' she replied.

It was time for sunrise, she held his hand, and they went to Sara's home. In the afternoon they woke up in each other arms. She knew that he was already married, and society will not accept this, she will be blamed for her doing.

She asked him, 'Aditya, if you're not happy with Meera, and if Meera too is living a compromising relationship, then both of you should get separated.'

He replied, 'It isn't as easy as it seems.'

'But a woman and man can find love even in the 40s and 50s. A career can start at the age of 45 too. Happiness can be found even at 50,' she said.

'Everything that you said is right, if me and my wife had to separate, we would have already. We have people in our relationship who are products of our love, our home, and it's our responsibility to protect them,' he replied, 'Sara I do love you, everything I said, is true, and from within.'

It was time to leave, he came closer and kissed her forehead. And bid goodbye.

It's been six years since then. Whenever Aditya thought of her first love, he always thought of the sunset at the seashore, that illuminating face. She had become a part of his imagination. Not for a single moment, he didn't think of her, but for him, his duties were a priority. One day, he received a letter.

Dear Aditya,

I knew this day would come. I don't dare to write this, but it's always you who gave me the one. I am not feeling confident, strong, or brave yet but have to do this and do everything to love myself again, collecting all my broken pieces to adjust them in a way no one will ever hurt me.

You left a void in me, and it will stay. I am not sure what comes next, but surely I'll figure it out. Maybe go back to NGO and start spending time with the orphans.

Time is very different here. It's good to be away from public ambitions.

I weekly go to watch the sunset thinking about you, the time we spent, the laughter we shared, the food you made, your jokes, and remember the love we have in between. I envy your wife that she had the chance to live with you…hahaha. Jokes apart I've spent all the time that I had left very well. I love you and will always do it till my last breath.

By the time you read this, I must have gone. See you on the other side.

Love

Sara

Sara had written this, a few months after Adi left Goa as she suppressed her wish to spend her remaining time with Adi. Thinking that, if Adi comes to know about her illness, he will leave his family and come to her, she hid the truth.

After receiving the news, Aditya broke down for the first time in his life. He was shattered and helpless. By now Sara had become a part of his life, although from a distance her existence was the cure to his otherwise, sad life.

The passing away of Sara changed him. His only motto was to live life to the fullest, as he learned it from her. To do the right thing, he started loving his family, and his wife more and more every day, until one day he loved his wife to the fullest.

Love never makes us weak, but strong. What is love, if it does not give you the strength to live alone? What is love, if it does not start from within? What is love, if it does not change you as a person? The love that Sara had for Aditya, didn't make her powerless, weak, and ill whilst making her strong to live with happiness in the time she had left with. Love is sacred, it is a sacrifice without thinking about oneself but for the good of others. Lucky are those who get the chance to live the love, and with whom they want they get to live with them.

19

A Bond Severed by Destiny

Upasana Hembram

March 2012

I was twelve years old and had been waiting for this day for weeks now because finally, my grandmother was going to move in with us. After I lost my grandfather last year, my father did not want my *Didima*, as I called her, to stay alone in the village. But it was a big decision and a lot of arrangements had to be made before my grandmother could agree. My parents and I spent the last few weeks cleaning out my room so we could fit in a new bed and a closet for my grandmother. I spent weekends drawing and painting and exhausted almost all the pages of my drawing book. I was so excited for her to see my drawings when she came. She was the biggest fan of my drawings. Her eyes would twinkle every time she looked at my artwork. Excitement kept bottling up inside me, and it was finally going to expel me today. I was busy giving the final touches to my grandma's new bed when the phone rang, and my mother picked it up, it was my dad on the line. They were on their way and would reach in half an hour or so. I started jumping with happiness. With the sound of every approaching car, I ran to the window by the front door and peeped outside to see If it was them. Every minute seemed like an hour. Finally, after what seemed like a zillion hours, my dad pulled up his car in the front yard. I opened the door and ran towards the car.

'Didima!' I cried. I was so happy to see that calm and wrinkly face again. Although she seemed pale from the time I had last seen her, her face lit up when she saw me.

'How are you, Munu?' she said smiling and giving me a warm hug.

'I am fine Didima, come in. I have lots to show you,' I picked up one of her bags and helped her come inside.

It took her a few weeks to settle down and adjust to our lifestyle, but it was nice having her. I no longer had to wait for vacations to see her; I could see her every day after school. She would wait for me by the window and greet my return with a hug every day.

'How was school? Did you finish your lunch box?' was a daily schedule question. The best part was our late-night talks on Fridays and Saturdays. On weekdays, she would insist on me sleeping early, but with the start of the weekend, she and I would sit down for hours and chat, I would pester her to tell me stories; some fictional and some from her childhood.

On one such weekend, after my parents had gone to their room, I sat near my grandma on her bed and asked her to tell me a story.

'I am out of stories, Munu. I don't know any more stories,' she said.

'Oh, come on, grandma. You have lived for so many years. Tell me anything. I am not sleepy,' I said.

'Why don't you tell me, what did you learn at school today,' she asked me while folding her clothes.

'Today, our geography teacher was not in the mood to teach. So, he asked us to share our adventures. My friends shared about their trips to various places. I too, shared about our trip to Jhargram, the zoo, and all about the jungles on the way,' I said.

'Ah! The jungles,' she sighed.

'It's a nice view, dense jungles on both sides of the road. Have you been to those jungles, Didima? They seem so spooky. I am sure there are wild animals too,' I asked her.

'Yes, and dacoits too,' she replied in a very low voice.

'Really!? You seem to know a lot about that place, don't you? Tell me, please,' I exclaimed.

She kept her folded clothes to the side and sat beside me, saying, 'I don't know a lot about the jungles, but an old friend did.'

I continued staring at her, my eyes begging for her to continue.

'It's an old story about a friend,' she said and sighed again.

'You know, I used to go to the school that is located after the jungle stretch. It was a small building when I was a kid, now it has three floors. There weren't many schools then. So, I had to walk for about 6 kms to reach school. Later, when I passed my matric exams, my father bought me a cycle,' she said.

'Whoa! You got a cycle after you passed your 10th standard,' I said in surprise, 'Dad gave me one when I passed my 4th standard.'

'Cycles were a luxury then, Munu. People would mostly walk,' she said.

'Oh! Then what happened? Did you have a lot of friends in school?' I asked.

'A few. We were a group of four girls. We would stick to each other throughout school hours. We sat on the same bench. There were boys too, but we would not talk to them. They were mischievous,' she said.

'Weren't you?' I asked.

'I was a shy girl, Munu. Kept to my business. But there was this one boy who, unlike others, was silent and did not speak much,' she said.

'Ooh, a boy finally!' I teased her.

She gave me a light tap on my shoulder and continued, 'One day afternoon, I was crossing those jungles, cycling back after school. Suddenly, the cycle's chain fell off and I had to stop. I was so afraid, and I did not know what to do. I did not even know how to fix it. I tried and tried but no use. After waiting for about 10 minutes, I realized it was better to start walking. So, I took my cycle and started walking home. After some time, I heard another cycle approach. I turned back and saw the same guy from class, the silent one. He got off his cycle and asked me what happened. I was surprised to hear his mellow voice. I showed him my cycle and the chain. He put his cycle on the stand and came over and fixed my cycle. From then on, we became friends,' she smiled.

'I introduced him to my friends the next day. We would have snacks together. Sometimes, my friends would be busy playing, but he and I would be talking. I liked it. I would sometimes feel that he told me all his secrets, and only then did I realize that he was not the introvert I had pegged him to be. He was a prankster too and played tricks on his siblings. Irrespective of that, he and I had a lot in common,' she continued.

I felt a change in tone in my grandmother's voice; from narrative to reminiscing. I tried to imagine as she continued.

'He used to live in the village next to ours, another half a kilometre towards the north. Sometimes, we would cycle back together. (*She paused*) There was this one time when I flunked my interim exams. My father threatened me and said he would get me married after my 11th if I did not do well. When I told him this, he helped me get my grades up. He was good at his studies. At some point, I began observing him closely. He was kind-hearted and helped anyone who asked. He respected our teachers and was well-mannered. It was difficult to find well-mannered guys. He also always encouraged me to study well,' she said in a go.

She took a pause, took a sip from her glass of water, and continued, 'I wanted him to meet my father. My father would have liked him. He always spoke of opening his shop and then growing it into a big business after his studies.'

'Then?' I asked.

'After a lot of thought and overcoming my fear, one Friday, I told my father about him and that I wanted to invite him for lunch. I will never forget that day; my father was so angry. He did not want to hear the rest of it, boys and girls weren't supposed to be friends then. The entire village would think badly of me. But my mother was different and forward-thinking. She agreed and promised me that she would convince your great-grandfather, and she did. I was so happy that he would come to my house. I could not wait to get to school on Monday and invite him. But he never came. He did not come the next day too. During the tiffin break, I saw a few teachers talking in the corridor. I heard them mention his name, so I went a bit closer. My math teacher was holding a Bangla newspaper; I could see a small picture of a boy. "Oh my god, it's him. He is in the papers!" I thought. I politely interrupted my teachers and asked for the paper. With the paper in my hand, I ran to the nearest empty classroom and read the article. 'Dacoit Activity Increases in Jhargram, Victim: A Youth' My heart dropped as I read on. On Sunday, he was cycling back from a wedding when a gang stopped him and tried to rob him. He fought back but was killed by one of the gang's armed robbers,' she finished and paused.

'What?' I jumped up and my eyes wide open, 'Killed?'

I could see my grandmother's eyes tearing up, but she controlled herself and wiped away the one drop that had decided to roll down her right cheek anyway.

'Yes, Munu. The news was then shared with our class in the second half. I came back home, and I cried myself to sleep that night,' she said.

'But grandfather died only last year?' I asked as I was a bit confused.

'I never said he was your grandfather. His name was Abhoy,' she sighed again.

There wasn't much left to talk about after this. I did not know what to tell her. I went to my bed and covered myself with a sheet. She did the same. I silently replayed the entire story in my mind. It played like a movie in front of my eyes. A boy and a girl met. A cupid strikes and the cycle chain goes bad. All those moments when they must have realized in their hearts that they were meant for each other. Moments that made their friendship special. Shy eyes, and butterflies fluttering in the stomach. But they never knew, even before they could confess to each other, that their love story would be cut short. Yes, even though I was a twelve-year-old, I realized that my grandmother had fallen for this 'boy'.

20

Anand—Heart Full of Smiles and Love

Chandni Ahuja

He wore his usual white shirt and a pair of royal blue Levi's jeans the last time I saw him wearing his benevolent smile. He was too shy and blushed when I smirked at his new military-cut look of salt and pepper. I will always love his natural look and never forget his beautiful smile.

I shall remember your words, 'to forever be fearless and gun down the animal inside me. I love you.'

-Drishti.

With hands full of shopping bags, Anand headed home. Little did he realize that it was the big day of his life, when he would meet someone extraordinary. He was taken to another city to meet a girl his age. Feeling exhilarated, Anand knocked on the door of that stranger. As the girl's sister opened the door, he froze. Anand thought that the beautiful young girl was the one. But he quickly realized that she was too young for him. When he stepped inside the house, he stared at the ceiling from which tiny scraps of paint hung around the corners. As Anand sat down on the chair after greeting the mother and everyone else in the family, his eyes met hers. He could not take his eyes off the beautiful woman standing right in front of him in a churidar. It was an obvious yes for Anand, who knew, maybe it was love at first sight for him. He fell in so deep for the lady named Aarti. When he stood up and was ready to leave, he had a moment of love where the two love birds stared at each other and smiled as if they knew they were destined to be together.

When things got serious, and families discussed tying knots to strengthen the bond, there came along a few misunderstandings. Anand's mother was bewildered to find a past acquaintance with her stepsister from Aarti's family, due to which she denied Anand's love. She wanted to break off the engagement, but Anand, who had only met the girl about once or twice, had fallen in love. He could not help but fight against his mum. His parents tried all the ways to get him to say no and instead marry off a wealthy woman, precisely a doctor. But he just couldn't. Anand stood for himself and stood bold and firm about his decision. He just had to marry Aarti. After several quarrels and bickering, his parents accepted his decision to see him happy. Anand felt excited about marrying the woman he loved so much in such a short time. It felt all magical for him when he envisioned growing old with her.

The day had finally arrived when they held themselves back from seeing each other before marriage as part of the Indian rituals. When Aarti slowly walked down the aisle and stepped up on the stage, Anand was stunned. He was astonished, looking at the young lady seeming so flawless and simple, yet so lovely. They smiled and giggled as they promised each other to be there in sickness and health, in richness and poorness. They tied knots and walked home together, holding hands tight.

It was very new for the young bride to settle into another house, let alone learn a new language, culture, and rituals. Aarti gradually adapted herself to the new city that Anand grew up in and loved so much. As days passed by, Aarti started to realize that Anand was too busy at work and did not seem quite as sweet as he used to be. She saw a different version of him, a version where he liked ogling other women for fun. Eventually, in a year, they had a beautiful baby girl. She seemed like she seized the heartbeat of her grandmother. The baby was named Drishti. She was loved a lot. Anand was attached to her and always did the best and even out of his league things to fulfill his daughter's needs and see a smile on her face. There came difficult times when Anand was on his own looking after his family. On heavy rainy nights, he ran down to the shop to buy nappies and cereals for the baby. Despite losing his slipper or seeing his bike sunk in rainwater, he kept walking home to make his baby sleep safe and sound.

Just two years down the line, Aarti faced something unexpected. Her father-in-law did not want her to live in his shelter anymore. Several bickering led to a strange storm. Anand was at fault, but he tried all ways to make his wife look bad. He complained about false things to his father to accuse his wife and leave her independently. When Aarti packed her bags and picked up the baby in her arms to return to the city she came from, she never realized it was forever. She felt that she could come back again when things were calm. But it was just the calm before the storm. Aarti tried calling her husband many times, but she only heard the robotic voice saying to try again. Phones were switched off, and accounts were deleted, leaving Aarti confused and scared.

One morning, Aarti's mum received a package delivered to their door. Aarti stood in tears to see the divorce papers. She did not perceive the forthcoming truth as she only saw her daughter's life and future ahead. It meant more than the love she had for her husband. After traveling on a local train with a handbag full of coins and a few clothes, Aarti tried to call her husband as her mother stood in anger and pain. Anand had left the house to live in a boy's hostel so people wouldn't suspect him of living under his father's shelter. Aarti had no choice but to sign the papers. Worrying about the whole life ahead, she signed them and picked her baby and promised to be the best mother and give the utmost love to her child. Picking up the bags and a few ornaments she had, Aarti travelled back to where she truly belonged.

Years passed as Drishti grew up to become a pretty girl with soft strands of hair hanging lose the whole day as she sat quietly inside the house, playing with the child-sized vessels and toys. She was fond of Barbie and pink-coloured dresses with shiny diamonds and rhinestones all over the edges. Drishti was fond of her mother and her father. She often spoke to him over the phone after her mother had some chit-chat.

Drishti always pleaded with her father to come and take her away as she couldn't bear the thought of not having her dad around all the time. Whenever she went to school, her friends and teachers asked for her dad's whereabouts. She missed having her dad see her win the karate competition, drawing competition, annual day, and sports day functions. Drishti smiled and wrote letters to her dad, wishing him to be happy and enjoy the occasion with a smile and love. In every tiny note she scribbled on, she requested her dad to come and take her and her mum. As much as Anand cherished and kept those colourful letters safe with him, he postponed her requests. He supposedly waited for an auspicious day to meet his family and reunite. Anand often tagged his friends along with him as he travelled somewhere to meet his ex-wife and his daughter. They always enjoyed themselves a lot and clicked many beautiful pictures of each other. Anand had a great bond with Drishti, but not in the way a usual father and a daughter had. Drishti was scared to call him her father after such a long time. She called him uncle as she never saw him live with her and her mum every day, every night. Drishti and Anand always sided together and planned a birthday party for Aarti; they ran out of the cute cottage and went out for a walk. She always sat on her father's shoulders and rode around new cities. Drishti was a lucky girl as her father loved her so much. He never denied a single wish of hers. If Drishti said she wanted the most beautiful but expensive glass shoes, her father bought them for her, despite her mother making frustrating faces. Drishti laughed off and happily cherished the times she spent with her father.

Only years later, Drishti and Aarti finally packed their bags to settle with Anand forever. Anand walked outside the airport in his city wearing cool shades and a big mustache. As Aarti and Drishti arrived at the airport, Drishti sat on the suitcase with her wide eyes staring at the city and people full of wonder. She wore a red and white top out of which tiny thread materials hung. Her father had pictured that day and locked it safe in his memory as he always recited that day to her. When Drishti tried adapting to the different weather and culture, she found herself lost and confused in the middle of the road. She parked her bicycle around the corner of a browser center shop, and even after reciting the road structure, she saw the other roads and confused herself. When Drishti called her father from a browsing shop, she cried and murmured to her dad. Anand laughed hard and asked her to wait just there. He drove on his bike and told her to follow him. He kept laughing and mocking her as she frowned.

Drishti, Anand, and Aarti spent a lot of time together in happiness and silence. There were many bitter times when she wondered who her father indeed was. When years later, a tiny baby was born, Drishti was left bewildered. She always wanted a baby sister and warned her mother that she would throw the baby in a bin if it were to be a boy. Ultimately, when she held the baby boy in a hospital, Drishti quickly melted. Her heart felt warm and heavy when she gently picked up the baby in her tiny arms. She looked at the baby's pink fingers and legs and kissed him. After numerous name discussions, the baby was named Aditya, as both Anand and Aarti loved that name.

It was a happy family of four. Drishti took care of her baby brother most of the time and kept him safe. She watched over him as he slept in peace and watched him as he woke up and peeped outside the swing with his huge sparkly eyes. Aditya had grown soft hair that his mother loved. Drishti and Aarti always picked him up and made tiny ponytails and plaits on his soft mushy hair. Anand was deeply attached to Aditya, more than ever. He wanted to change for the better. But, the circumstances were different, and he had become a different person over the years of living without his wife and daughter. There was a seemingly obvious distance between Drishti and Anand, but it was okay. The three kept themselves occupied as Anand left for work early in the morning. He always woke his daughter up early so she could study and be healthy. Regardless of her sulking, Drishti woke up and walked around the balcony to hear the chirping of the birds and look at the milkman dropping off the packets at each house in the neighbourhood.

Time flew as Drishti and Aditya grew up. There were great times when their father took the family to travel abroad. But there were also times when the kids heard the shackling and breaking voices of their mothers. Alcohol was the most terrible mistake a person ever makes in life, and Anand could not help it. He was so addicted to it that he could go to the moon if he had to get it. It brought out an ugly personality of his that his family hated. It broke Aarti and Drishti to watch him in pain. When Drishti tried several ways and made him promise several times, Anand shoved her away. In the process of him being broken inside out, he broke those two inside out. Drishti dreamt of having a beautiful house and living with her family happily. Seeing such difficult circumstances, she understood that every human had their share of pain and suffering. She just wanted to end all the suffering her family faced and find the love for her father that she always sought.

One day, Anand felt like he was a lost cause who always left his loved ones hurt. He felt sorry and apologized to his wife and daughter. He stood in front of them and burst into tears. Drishti never heard the word sorry out of his mouth for all the badmouthing, and she cried. She wiped off her tears and instructed her dad to sit down on the chair. As Aarti and Anand wondered what she was doing, she stood around the dining room and sobbed. Her father picked up her hand and pulled her in. He made her sit on his lap as she struggled to speak and murmured, 'Thank you.' She had never seen him meltdown like this, and she confessed that all the pain and trauma had disturbed her since childhood. Drishti had matured, and she understood the difficult times. She smiled at him as her father wiped off her tears and cracked a silly joke to make her laugh.

Times were different, and every person in the family shared their part of the pain. They stood by each other through everything. But, one fine morning, when Aarti received an emergency call to leave the city and look after her sister, she panicked. Anand walked into the dark bedroom, where Drishti peacefully slept around 9 in the morning. He called her out and told her to pick up her mum's phone. Soon Aarti and the kids packed their bags to go over and look after her younger sister. When Anand happily dropped them off at the station, Drishti took a deep breath from the car around 3 in the morning. Aditya hugged his dad as Anand bid goodbye to his wife, and suddenly, Drishti looked back and smiled at him. She saw him drive away in the car and walk towards the train. A few days later, Aarti and her kids rushed back home when Anand stopped picking up phone calls from anyone. Aditya fell to his knees to find that his dad had died. Aarti froze and panicked as she kept murmuring that she was scared to see him. Drishti could not accept the truth and cried with pain and fear inside her aching heart. She could not accept the truth about his father, who always spoke highly of everyone; he just took away his life.

***

Anand was a bright and brilliant man living his mid-aged life. He was happy and an extraordinary man who held no grudges against anybody. Anand always stood out as being the first person when someone needed help. Anand was always in service to people around him as he saw every human as his own family. He never expected anything in return but love and blessings. Drishti was pissed off at his father, who was such a beautiful soul, telling everyone not to give up so easily. He always explained to Drishti to live her life the way she wanted to and tell people to fuck off.

Anand uttered the words, 'Only thing that you value, you shall recognize as a treasure. And only what you treasure, you will take care of it so that you never lose it.' When Drishti saw glimpses of her father in a dream, she raised her voice and frowned at him, asking for a note. When she saw her father smile and tell her, 'Bittu, you'll find it, I'm telling you,' She was confused. All the questions and no answers about what was her future, what was her mother's future, and what was her little brother supposed to do, she kept wondering, feeling off.

At one point, Drishti prayed for her father to be at peace and away from all the assholes in the surrounding who troubled him so much. When she returned from her father's office, she sat in the rickshaw with tears rolling down her cheeks as she astonishingly found a note in her father's office. She rushed to her bedroom and read it to her mother. When she read him apologizing to everyone for his mistakes and saw the final words of the note saying that he was grateful for three beautiful souls; his children and his wife, who made it happen, it brought tears to her eyes, making her hands shiver. Drishti loved her father and kept his note safe inside a file stacked with precious souvenirs and greeting notes. She held no grudges but tried coping with regrets in her heart. She now remembers and cherishes the thought that she was and always will be her father's mischievous gorgeous princess who sat on the edge of a huge suitcase wearing a crocheted red and white top and blue jeans, with eyes full of wonder seeking love and care. Drishti knew that no matter how bold of a woman she turned out to become, she would always be that quiet and cute little daughter of her pops.

Drishti just wanted to see him smile the last time and say that he was proud of her. She never wanted to see his charming and handsome father taking his last breath between four walls. Anand always told his family that he was a ferocious and brave lion who incessantly roared outside and ran around with freedom. That thought deeply hurt her and made her feel bad and confused. She wondered whether he would've picked up his shattered pieces and mended them with grace had they not abruptly left the city in the middle of the night due to an emergency. She somehow accumulated her thoughts as she bid him goodbye with love and bright red tearful eyes. She wished to have dinner with him at the table and hug him one last time and tell him that the world wasn't with him, but his family was. With all her cluttered thoughts and love for him, she sketched his smiling face and kissed it. He had a bright smile with a dark mustache and a shimmering earring in one ear. The photo was the young image of him that reminded everyone of what a gold-hearted man he always was. She safely pinned the photo of him inside a file. Aarti, Aditya, and Drishti stood firm and held onto the good memories as he left the cruel world to be in peace. Ultimately, destiny glued the family even tighter than before with beautiful memories of Anand. It was time for the three of them to step outside and stand up for themselves without fearing societal approval. They finally picked up their courage to fight against the world for what was rightfully theirs with the hope that everything would get better over time.

21

The Chain Snatcher

Aniket Gauns

Lokesh, a skinny, 20-year-old guy, was standing on the edge of a cantilever bridge, which stood at a huge height above a beautiful river. With him, are his 10 friends, standing at equal distances on the bridge, with ropes in their hands. With the sound of an approaching train, Lokesh signalled everyone to tie the ropes. Everyone started tying one end of the rope to their waist and the other to the big, solid bars of the bridge. Lokesh tied an extra knot to support his left foot, which was injured. Ramesh, Lokesh's best friend was next to him. The view from the bridge was beautiful. People traveling in trains waited especially for the arrival of the bridge. Passengers, tend to stand at the train doors, with their phones or witness the utter beauty of the scenery from their windows. The bridge, offers the most exquisite image at this time, the sunset.

Before the first wheel of the train hit the bridge, people were already at the doors. Lokesh and the gang were hiding behind the big bars of the bridge. Their slim bodies were barely noticeable to the passengers. As the train crossed half the bridge, the gang, out of their hiding, stretched their bodies towards the train. With the ropes supporting them, they snatched everything they could from the passengers. By the time train crossed the bridge, passengers had lost their phones, wallets, and even their gold chains. It was a win for the gang. Lokesh alone managed to snatch a phone and a chain.

It was evening and the gang had come to meet Deepak, their dealer. Everyone handed over their catch to Deepak. His base was in the same poor neighbourhood, where these boys belonged to. He employed these kids to rob and snatch, for which he paid them their share. Lokesh was Deepak's most trusted player, an expert in train snatching. But one fine day, Lokesh, gave him only the phone and kept the chain for him. He then came home and gave some money to his single mother, who was unwell and had left her job. Lokesh was the breadwinner of the family.

The next day, Lokesh was sitting with a girl, in the middle row of the classroom. They had an innate chemistry, which would take the attention of anyone entering the room. Geeta's notebook was filled, while Lokesh just had an empty notebook. The teacher spotted Lokesh flirting and asked him a question. To everyone's surprise, he answered it correctly, thanks to Geeta who prompted answers. The class ended and everyone left. The teacher approached Geeta and warned her not to engage much with Lokesh. To which Geeta replied, 'Ma'am, I am just helping him in his studies.'

The teacher was annoyed with her reply.

Lokesh swiftly placed the gold chain in Geeta's hand. She was shocked and elated. Geeta was curious to know how he got the chain. But instead, he avoided the question and asked her to hurry for her football practice, and both left.

At football practice, Geeta played as the forward for the college team. Lokesh was a spectator. The game ended in a draw, where Geeta missed an easy chance to score. She was frustrated and felt low. Lokesh tried to console her and promised to train with her, every day, till the finals.

Geeta asked him, 'Why did you stop playing football?'

He showed her, his left foot, which got injured, and that he could not play at full intensity now. Geeta noticed Lokesh's eyes lying but tried to avoid further discussion.

After leaving the ground, both of them met Lokesh's friends at a tea stall. Lokesh and Ramesh smoked a cigarette. They invited Geeta to the village fair, which used to happen once a year. Lokesh did not want Geeta to see the poor neighbourhood he came from, he tried to avoid it, by reminding Geeta of their football practice.

But Geeta was eager to see Lokesh's village, and she expressed her huge love for Ferris wheel rides.

'I want to sit with you on a Ferris wheel,' she said. Lokesh finally agreed, and all were excited to show Geeta their village.

At the village fair, Geeta wore a white Punjabi ethnic suit. Her long-braided hair and the gold chain on the neck looked magical. Lokesh was yet to arrive, as everyone was about to enter the Ferris wheel. As Geeta was about to sit on the ride, Lokesh came running out of nowhere and sat beside her. The wheel ride started, and Geeta shouted her lungs out. Lokesh loved the sheer joy on her face. He held her hand mid-air, bringing her closer and Geeta stopped shouting. The time stood still as they shared a passionate kiss. This was their first kiss, and it was euphoric. The Ferris wheel ride ended. Geeta and Lokesh had bright smiles on their faces. Just then, a few policemen rush towards them and nabbed Lokesh and Ramesh by their collars. Nobody had any clue about what just happened.

At the police station, Deepak bailed out Lokesh and Ramesh, by bribing the police. Lokesh and Ramesh leave the police station and see Geeta waiting outside. Geeta confronted Lokesh and asked him to explain, she was scared. When Lokesh tells her why he was arrested, Geeta was in shock. Lokesh explains to her the conditions at his home and that he is the only bread earner. Geeta could not comprehend anything at that moment.

'Quit this thing if you want to be with me,' she said.

Lokesh agreed and promised.

'Lokesh, where did this gold chain come from?' she asked.

Lokesh was in tears, and he told her the train-snatching truth. Geeta was devastated. She removed the chain, handed it over to Lokesh, and started walking away as he stood there helpless.

The next day, Lokesh met Deepak, expressing his wish to retire from this kind of work but Deepak was reluctant. A long confrontation happened when Lokesh decided that he won't turn back no matter what Deepak said. However, to his surprise, Deepak asked him to repay the bail money that he bribed, if he wishes to quit. He did not have money even to feed his mother at home. Deepak then offered Lokesh to do one last robbery for him. This time, not from a train but from his rival builder, who wanted to demolish one of Deepak's projects. Lokesh asked for some buffer time to think about this.

The next day, Lokesh was with Geeta on the football ground, he placed Geeta's hands in his and told her that he had given up on the job and wanted to start a new life with her. Geeta was happy. Lokesh wanted Geeta to win the finals of the college tournament and Geeta promised to do so. Both trained all night for the match.

On the day of the final, Lokesh met her at the college gate. While they were walking, Lokesh got a call from Deepak, and he disconnected immediately. While Geeta told him about how stressed she is, Lokesh interrupted him and said, 'I have to go for some work.'

Geeta was clueless. 'I forgot to give Mom her medicines,' he said.

'But I need you to be here, Lokesh,' she said.

Lokesh assured her that he would reach on time and that nothing will stop her from winning the match. He bid bye to Geeta in a hurry and leaves.

***

Lokesh and Ramesh were waiting outside a bank, on a motorbike. Lokesh improvised the plan by saying to Ramesh that he should drive instead, and Ramesh should snatch the bag. Ramesh warned him that his injured foot might cause problems while rushing the bike, but Lokesh was reluctant. He had promised Geeta that he would not snatch anything, and he felt he should be riding the bike. Ramesh agreed and they switched roles.

The builder came out of the bank with his bodyguards and walked towards his car. Lokesh raced the bike towards him and right when they passed him, Ramesh snatches the bag from his hand, and they zip past them. At a distance from the builder's car, a traffic signal shows yellow light. Lokesh tried to put the bike lever in a higher gear, but Lokesh's injured left leg gave way. In his attempt to forcefully shift the gear, the bike did not pace up, the signal turned red. Lokesh tried to race past the signal but, an elderly man on a bike, from the opposite junction, had already left his mark. Lokesh, trying to dodge crashed into it, and both were heavily injured.

While people helped the other man, the builder and his bodyguards caught Ramesh and Lokesh. They are heavily beaten and later an ambulance took them to the hospital. A few days later, Lokesh's mother, Geeta, and an injured Ramesh along with others, were standing at the bridge. As the passengers clicked pictures of the scenery from the bridge, Geeta and Lokesh's mother immersed the ashes of Lokesh into the river. Ramesh's fate ended at the bridge.

22

Buried Soul

Vijila M

The sun came over our heads, I tried to look, but I couldn't raise my eyes toward it. It was a sunny day. I was at a bus stop. It was crowded, I exclaimed, where the people are going on such a hot sunny day. I tried to protect my foot from the heat emitted from the tar and unfortunately, I caught into the crowd. Each one was sweating and wiping their face, flowing swept through their face and neck. I had a bath just an hour ago, but I felt like a deep-dried fish under the hot sun. My wet tissues too became useless. Like others, my handkerchief also got wet. The heat from the sun could help me with drying my handkerchief, but there was no way I would show it to the sun in a crowded place. I felt water springs on my body, sweat running through all parts of my physic. Fewer trees on the roadside, and the hot air made it even tougher for me.

In front of me, across the road, was a masque and people were coming out of it after the mass. They wore long white kurtas and caps over their heads, neat and perfect clothes. It was around half past 1 in the afternoon, and some kids around were playing while some were hungry.

Out of nowhere, a charming face smiled at me in front of the gate, from the masque. I stared for a while and recognized him. It was Hussain; tall, fair, curly-haired, good and handsome, he wore a white long kurta and white cap. He took off his cap, started to walk towards me, two steps ahead, and was intruded on by someone. He signalled me to stay for a while. I looked for my bus and prayed to come quickly before he reaches my side.

I have known him for two years, through one of my friends. They fell in love with each other. To me, they were the best couple, the perfect pair I had ever seen. Their journey was like a fantasy tale. The only difference between them was religion. He was from a traditional Muslim family, and she was from a deep routed Christian family.

I don't know what he was doing now, but they broke up three months ago. I heard that he injured himself with a knife, through one of his friends.

The person was about to move, and he smiled at me. They hugged each other and bid byes, he smiled at me, and my eyes turned to the side, to look for my bus. I was unfortunate.

He walked towards me. I didn't know what to say. I too stepped out of the bus stop and stood under a tree that had only three small branches and it didn't provide any shade.

'Hi,' he said, walking across the road.

'Hi,' I murmured with a smile and waved at him.

He approached closer.

'How are you?' I asked.

'Yeah, going, how are you doing?' he asked.

'I'm good,' I paused with a grin.

We both fell short of words and felt a little nervous, I was sure he would enquire about her. And deep inside I wished for my bus to arrive soon. Many buses came but I was waiting for a woman's special, free-of-cost bus. I decided to board any bus which will come next.

'Where are you going? This time?' he asked.

With hesitation, 'To my aunt's house,' I said.

Because her house is next to my aunt's house, I could see a flare of interest in his eyes and he was about to ask something, I ignored him and looked for the bus.

'How is she?' he asked, 'after that incident.'

'Not bad, recovering slowly,' I wanted to stop the conversation.

'Did she tell anything to you?' he asked.

I couldn't understand his situation and I was not interested in answering him.

'Yes, she is very adamant in her decision, she is not ready to give up for anyone's sake. Is it enough for you?' I raged a little.

His face went down, 'It is an injustice to me,' he murmured, 'it is injustice for her too.'

'Hmm. She accepted for herself, but I couldn't,' I paused.

He didn't dare to reply.

'Why did you sign, at the police station?' I asked him.

He said nothing, he tried several times to explain his point, but it was too late, my friend was about to become a Nun. Still, I didn't know whether she was really happy or if she had anything else on her mind.

Her parents also accepted her decision, to prevent their daughter to marry a Muslim boy.

'Can you do me a favor?' he asked, hesitantly.

I was confused, 'Tell, if I can,' and wished it should not be about her.

'Can you make her call me?' he continued 'Once, only one time!'

'I am not sure' I replied, 'It depends on the situation, because she is recovering slowly. I cannot see her depressed again.'

'Try for once please, what can I do more than that?' He stumbled. His face became dull, and his eyes filled with tears, he dare not to shed it in public, he controlled it.

I knew he was struggling but she also does so, who could I support? So, I decided to stand out of the frame.

'See, it's you, who have decided to part, at first, now what will she do? Do you expect her to come again and crave your love?' I spoke.

'No not like that,' he continued, 'I want her to change her decision.'

I said nothing, he bid bye to me, and I waved to him, he left.

I was angry. It was all his fault. They knew their family won't accept their love, so he asked her to come out of the house, only to get married in the registered office. She did so, but his father got to know it somehow and, their marriage was unsuccessful. Her parents charged a case against Hussain. So, the police arrested him, they tried to pacify both of the families, but they didn't.

Her parents were ready to accept Hussain if he converts to Christianity, but Hussain's family would not. To them, they wanted the relationship to end. They were not ready to accept, a girl from another religion, stepping into their family. Hussain was ready to come out of his house to marry her, but fate, her parents persuaded her not to do so. This time she was confused and did not dare to leave her parents.

Finally, after a day's trial, the police asked them to sign to break the relationship. She said no and he did too. But after Hussain's family persuaded him to sign, he did it. She signed too. They both left the police station, having signed copies of the paper, in their hands.

I never wondered how a single sheet of paper could stop them, from loving each other.

The bus came; the crowd was squeezing to board. Somehow I managed to get into the bus. The dust went off in a heap; I held my breath for a little while and went back to normal. I did it, I boarded.

'How many?' the conductor asked.

'One,' I said.

He gave me one ticket; the sun showed no mercy, and the crowded bus emitted more heat.

However, as I reached my stop, I walked and reached my aunt's house.

'Why didn't you bring an umbrella?' asked my aunty 'Direct exposure to sun rays might cause skin problems.'

'Okay, aunt.' I replied, 'I forgot.'

I gave the bags to her; after a cold shower, I felt rid of the heat. My aunt gave me a cup of lemon juice; she poured salt instead of sugar. I felt energetic.

'Aunty,' I shouted, 'I am going to Grace's house, and will be back in five minutes.'

'Okay!' She replied from the kitchen, 'Come soon.'

'Okay!' I spoke.

Grace's father sat on the steps, doing nothing, thinking something. Her mother welcomed me.

'How are you Nithya?' asked Grace's mother.

'I am doing good, Aunty,' I replied.

She directed me to Grace's room and asked me whether I need any drinks.

'No Aunty, I just had lemonade a minute ago,' I said.

'Okay, ask me if you need anything,' she said.

'Sure,' I replied.

I knocked on Grace's door.

'Come, the door is open,' said Grace in a thin voice, and asked, 'How are you dear?'

'I am good. How are you doing?' I asked.

'Yeah, doing well,' she replied.

I had no other words. I sat in front of her and saw her face glowing with divinity. I tried not to speak about him now; I didn't want to make her dull, same time I didn't like her decision, to become a Nun. She had many dreams before.

'Grace… um' I stumbled, 'I saw…'

She intrudes me, 'How is your study going?'

'Yeah, going good' I decided not to speak about Hussain.

A while later, I decided I should go. She asked me to stay for a while, but I hesitated and left.

She took one book, which was religious, and started to read it, her fingers were busy with the rosary beads. I left her house, with a heavy heart.

Still, I can't understand how a signed paper will put an end to all emotions of the soul. Or else did they bury their emotions under their religion's principles?

23

Farewell to My Freestyle Dive

Esther Graciya G.

'Still sleeping, wake up butter girl, you know where you have to be in a few minutes from now,' Dad said.

'Hmm! Dad, I will get up in a just,' Pat said and slammed her head to the pillow kept next.

Dan walked to the bed and pulled the sheets away. 'Get up dear, it's already late,' he said tapping her cheeks.

Pat looked at her watch, rushed towards the door, grabbed her toothbrush, and got ready for the day in a hurry.

Meanwhile, Dad was busy preparing her some breakfast and suddenly the phone rang.

'Hi honey, what is it?' Dan said as his wife called.

'Dan can't you converse slightly more, most of the time when she is late you ask me what is it first and never listen to me, remember the first person who calls has something to say or ask, but I always end up listening to you and ending calls. Funny I wonder why I called,' she ranted.

'I don't know, (*He laughed*) I used to do that a lot,' he said.

'Dan, even you are tired from hearing me speak, right?' she asked.

'No! No… Hmm! Well, I just told you, you talk a lot, especially when our daughter has a lot of training schedule, please try to understand this,' Dan said.

'Dan, sometimes you act busy, so spend some time with me. You and Pat spend more time together than you spend time with me,' she said.

'Alright, I'm sorry, but can we talk about this later? It's late already,' Dan said.

'I can leave a loose tie, just because it is a leave from Pat's academics. Take some space,' she said.

'Okay, darling. You take your leave and whenever you want I'll support you dearly,' Dan said.

'Dan? Nice then. I'll plan my biggest vacation soon,' she said.

'Sure dear, I can handle that for you. I have to go,' Dan said.

'Okay Dan, bye,' she said and hung up the call.

Plating the breakfast, he knocked on the door, 'Pat! Pat! Come on.'

'Dad! Just a second,' she said and opened the door.

'Hmm,' she said taking the plate, 'thanks, Dad.'

'Have them, should I get your coffee too?' Dan asked.

'Dad, did you have yours?' Pat asked.

'No, not yet, I was on a call with your dear mother,' he said.

'Hehe,' she giggled. 'Dad, I suggest you can go and see Mom in your free time, or vacation will also do,' Pat said.

'Yeah, it's been a while since she came home, I'd love her to take a break,' he said.

'Okay! Come here Dad,' she said while Dan was putting on his shirt.

'Wait, the ironed shirt will get crushed, hold my hand instead,' he said.

'Okay, sit here, I'll get your coffee, have it first,' Pat said.

'Thanks, dear,' Dan said.

'Dad, which song have you been listening to lately?' Pat asked while she poured some water into the kettle.

'Would you listen to my playlist, Pat?' Dan asked with uncertainty.

'No, not the entire playlist, but that one special song from your playlist that you listen to untimely,' Pat said and walked towards her dad, and gave him her phone to enter the song name.

'Sure dear,' he paused and continued, 'Hmm! it's tough to write just one. But here, guess who it is from by just listening. I'll give you something.'

'Well, Dad you're drawing me in on a deal,' she replied as she added some grounded coffee powder to the brewing machine and poured some hot water.

With the smell of hot steam from the coffee decoction, 'Hmm... I guess, Dad this song is country style?' Pat asked.

'Yeah! And guess the singer?' Dan said.

'I think it's a lady who's singing, Murphy's is it, Dad?' Pat asked.

'Yeah! That's right, how do you remember it?' Dan asked.

"You have played it in the car countless times,' Pat said.

'Ohh. I assumed you used your headphones a lot, don't you?' Dan asked.

'Surprised, aren't you? I love your music taste too, Dad,' she said and smiled.

'Dear Pat, come here!' he called her.

She walked towards her dad and hugged him tightly. 'Deal, Dad?' (*She paused*), 'What is it you will give me?'

In a hurry, Pat tried to snuggle out of the hug, but just then her dad gave her a loud kiss on the cheeks.

'Dad, I could hear you kiss. It's echoing in my ears already,' Pat said.

'I know you're growing up fast, but can't I kiss my daughter at home?' Dad asked.

'You have stopped and only do it on my birthday,' she replied, 'Dad, even though I don't kiss you every day, I still love you.'

'Pat, dear I love you too, even though I don't say it out loudly,' Dan said.

'I do Dad. I'll get your coffee,' Pat said as Dad sat on the chair nodding his head with a smile.

She poured some milk in decoction and the aroma drifted through, only for Pat to levitate blankly.

'Pat, daydreaming dear?' He asked, 'It's funny how you had it since you were small.'

'Oh. Sorry did I do it again?' Pat asked realizing she was dreaming.

'No problem dear, but you have to reheat it again so, I am worried about that, I can drink it however it is, but you like your coffee warm right?' Dan asked.

'Yeah, Dad, I break my stress with caffeine,' Pat replied.

'What were you stressed about lately?' Dad asked with concern.

'Your kiss Dad,' she replied with a laugh.

'Really! Dear, I would not do that again,' Dad replied.

'Dad, you can kiss me no problem. I was just kidding,' Pat giggled shaking her head, 'I don't know what to choose.'

'Pat you are young dear, you don't have to figure it out now. But the important thing is you try out things, not for the future; to just try various aspects of life,' Dan said, 'think Pat, how you ended up only with black current, there are other flavors right?'

'I tried every one of them, so I had time to taste every flavour, one at a time, and found the one flavour palate better,' she said.

'See? Great, it is time, so you're trying flavors, which stand out with you on all ground 360 degrees involving not only passion but strength, emotion, endurance, goal, and opportunity. Measure all of this in satisfaction then it will help you to decide, for now just taste the flavors for life,' Dan said.

'Dad, you should have become a counselor,' Pat teased him.

'That's off-limits,' Dan said, 'and, we have to leave after sipping coffee.'

'Sure Dad, but it's not warm.' Pat replied.

'Have it here, or you can buy yours on the way,' Dan said, 'or keep this one in the fridge.'

'I'll just have a sip now, later re-heat, and having coffee will be a delight from head to toe,' Pat said, 'It will feel like conquering warmth all over again.'

'A great start for an evening dear, okay that can wait on the slab there, cover it with a plate, Pat. (*He paused*) I'll get your bags and go to the car. Make sure you lock the door and bring the keys without forgetting,' Dan said.

In the car, Dan waited for Pat.

'There, we can be on time. Glad that I found your coaching right here, otherwise it would have been a problem,' Dan said.

'Dad I know you're talking about being late. We can be there on time, you're the best driver, remember?' Pat asked sitting in the front seat.

'Pat, I was a racer back then, now I'm more than a half-century old and I can't over-speed!' Dan said, 'It's crucial for you and the state, I can't get a speeding ticket again.'

'Okay Dad, just drive, we can make it on time, and can't wait to see the coach's face when a last-second tick and he sees me behind him,' Pat said.

'Haha! Pat, you always like this, I can't forget,' Dan said.

'The look, right Dad?' Pat asked.

'Yes, dear,' Dan replied.

'I can't stop laughing over this,' she laughed.

'Pat calm down I'll lose the grip,' Dan said.

'Okay!' she said.

'Dad, can I have coffee now?' she asked after a pause.

'I'll try to stop there, it's right here in this corner I guess. There, I'll get them for you, stay right here,' he instructed.

'Sure,' she said.

At the coffee shop,

'Good morning sir, what would you like to order?' the order taker asked.

'Usual coffee, I'll go to the counter and pay,' Dan said.

'Sure sir, it will be ready on the go,' the person said.

As he picked up the coffee, 'Thank you as always, and have a blessed day ahead,' Dan said.

'Thank you, sir, and wish you the same,' the cashier said.

As he approached the car, 'Hmm! Espresso or cappuccino?' Pat asked Dan.

'You guess dear,' Dan said as he sat in the driver's seat.

'I think it's the usual one,' Pat said.

'How do you know?' Dan asked.

'Well, see that bike their Dad, it means the order taker is already there so, it's easier to give an order through him,' Pat replied.

'Hmm. I smell suspicion!' he said.

'Dad nothing is going on. You'll know when I like someone,' Pat said.

'Sure, I'd like to be the first one to hear about it,' Dan said.

'Indeed,' she said, 'I'll have mine here.'

'Sure, I'll keep it for the later company,' Dan said.

'Yeah, it takes an hour and a half hours of practice, completing it will make me feel great,' she said, 'Dad I'll miss going there as it's about to end.'

'Come on Pat, you can go to practice at your hometown riverside, it's beautiful and also quite scenic in admiration,' Dan said.

'I can admire beauty in time there,' she said, 'Mom loves to come back there.'

'Dad, I can come back for my friends, I miss them like winter warmth, especially in a new city.' she continued, 'I do chat though.'

'Pat, call them, there is no better conversation than talking over the phone. Listening to your buddies' stories grabs time and memories together,' Dan said.

'Wow! It is a great way to put words like that, it makes me want to listen to you,' Pat said.

'It brings a smile too, you look like a happy soul, my dear Pat,' Dan said.

'Yeah Dad, talking makes the time fly,' she said.

'Pat, you are a funny mood destroyer. One thing I remember is when we as a family had gone to May's wedding, Mom and I kept talking to guests. You came in and pulled me over and said you're sick and Mom left the conversation immediately. I can't stop laughing it was so real,' Dan said.

'Dad, you remember it, I thought I was not caught,' she said laughing as she sipped coffee.

'You can't fool me,' Dan said.

'I'm done with the coffee, we can go I can't wait to see coaches eye,' she said.

'Indeed, I do too dear, okay buckle up,' Dan said.

Pat adjusted the seat belt, plugged in her ear pods, and played music on the go. Driving the car, en route, Dan started humming to the tune of the song from the radio. Pat noticed this, she smiled and continued watching the birds and the scenery outside. The way some people enjoyed life with minimum resources, fascinated her.

'Ready to stir coach reaction, Pat,' Dan asked as he took a sharp turn on a bridge.

'Yes!' she said.

'Alright, I'll park it right there. Just hang on, you have a minute,' Dan said.

'Meanwhile, I'll get set,' she said.

'Sure,' Dan replied.

'I'll go to the back door, you come in the front and then you can get a good glimpse of the coach,' she said laughing, 'See ya.'

She waited behind the coach as the coach looked at his waterproof wristwatch. Dan approached the front door with his phone camera on, signalling Pat a smile of readiness for the scene.

Pat stood there ready and offered her hand in front of the coach, and smiled, as the coach still looked at his watch.

With eyes big in surprise, 'Pat, you always make me wait till the last millisecond, don't you?' Coach asked.

'You always get surprised at my timing right?' Pat asked laughing.

'I hope you learn to swim freestyle,' Coach said.

'Will coach,' Pat said.

'Try to hold your breath longer as you kick, look at me, and move your hands at this angle,' Coach was guiding her.

After practicing for minutes, Pat shouted, 'Dad, I did it,' as Dan recorded it.

Looking above the water, she saw someone at a distance and felt strange. Seeing that boy approaching the water she rushed to the dressing room.

As she went to the car, she overheard the boy's dad talking to the coach, seeking approval for a month's leave, as they had to travel for a business meeting.

'Pat, come here,' Coach called her, 'I'm happy for your spirit, stay like this.'

Pat smiled and they clicked a picture together.

'Thanks, Coach,' Pat said.

As she walked, her smile reduced, and she heard some footsteps following behind.

With a strange feeling of excitement and lessons of caution crossing her mind, she wanted to turn around, but couldn't.

The boy's dad called him back,

'It's a no, my son, you have to train somewhere else,' his dad said.

As the footsteps stopped, Pat looked back at him and looked back, sat in the seat, and wondered with a feeling so strange; yet drawn towards the thought.

'Pat, a warm hug from coffee, right?' Dan asked.

She nodded saying yes.

Meet the Co-Authors

Chandni Ahuja (*~Chandi*)

Chandni hails from Pune and is an English literature graduate who is passionate about writing poetry. She loves to imagine characters from real-life experiences. She is a firm believer in magic and hope. Her faith in standing with her people makes her an empathic person. She finds peace in baking and enjoys learning more about baking along with a hot cup of coffee in her me time. Her goofiness and silence confuse everyone, but she predicts the right people who understand her inside out and tends to stay true to them.

Vanitha Murugan

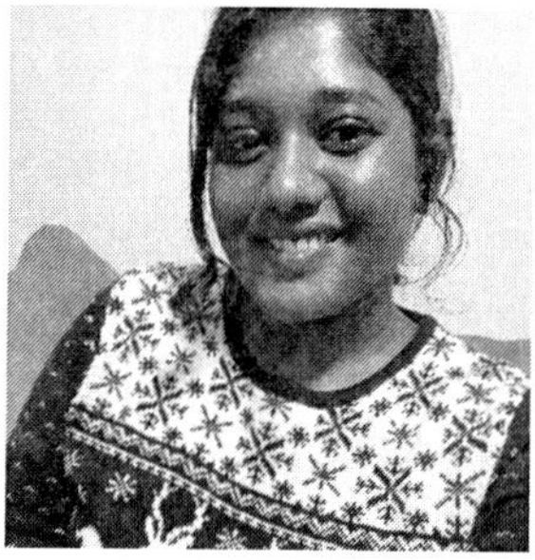

Vanitha from Madurai (TN) started penning down her thoughts during her school days, which eventually led her way to become a passionate writer. She is a Biotechnology graduate from Anna University and pursuing Cancer research at the University of Glasgow. Other than Found and Lost, she has also participated in an anthology named "Feelings of Love". In her me time, she reads and plays with her pet.

Surya Sai Prasanth Palaparthy

Brought up in Hyderabad, Surya Sai Prasanth is an introvert and an amateur writer/poet. He is a big movie buff and a F.R.I.E.N.D.S. fanatic. He is not great at advice, but he can interest you in a sarcastic comment. He loves talking about science fiction stuff like time travel. Weirdly enough, he has a favorite spider species.

Esther Graciya G.

Esther hails from the capital city of the beautiful state of Karnataka, Bangalore. Passion for writing is her innate quality and she is the first one in her family to become a published writer. Encouragement and quality time with her loved ones make her life speak and open up. Even though her personality is different, such experiences influence her life and appreciate people. Her writings can be seen on her Instagram page, @theegg_officially

Mahek Thakar

Mahek Thakar is an Indo-Canadian author. With dual degrees in Literature and Music, she has a fine blend of Teaching, Singing, and Writing. She lived in Ahmedabad for 7 years and moved to Toronto in 2019. Mahek considers Love, Friends, and Family to be most important

to her. She spends most of her time exploring new places and bringing new experiences from those trips into her journal. She loves to pen short stories and fiction based on people, places, experiences, spirituality, and philosophy. Found and Lost holds the first piece of her contribution to the Literary World.

Upasana Hembram

Upasana is a simple girl with big dreams. Hailing from the small town of Kharagpur, West Bengal, she aspires to travel the world one day. In her quiet time, she loves reading or watching suspense thrillers or creating imaginary worlds on the pages of her notebook. She is a budding writer who is inspired by real-life or close-to-her-heart events.

Vijila M

Vijila belongs to the Kanyakumari district in the state of Tamil Nadu. She graduated in literature. 'The Buried Soul' is her first published short story in English. She writes genres like poetry, short stories, and novels in both Tamil and English languages. She notices the differences in the world and deals with Destiny's directions in people's lives. She writes down all her observations about society and directs the readers into her imaginary world.

Dr. Sanjana Venkatraman *(~homosapien94)*

Sanjana is a dentist, writer, and human being who is always looking for a deeper meaning in life. She enjoys her time being creative and uses writing as a way to express herself. She likes stories and the value they bring. She believes everyone's life is a story and can be so deep and meaningful. She is also passionate about setting herself free through dance. Her writings can be seen on her Instagram page @homosapien94.

Ishat Sharma

Ishat is a boy from the mountains. He was born in a district of Jammu province, Udhampur. His life revolves around his family, and he finds joy in little things, listens to his inner voice, and believes in breaking the stereotypes. He believes only you're your strongest competitor and no one else. Ishat believes in the fact that sometimes you fall in love at the least expected times when the stars ain't aligned. But some paths are meant to be crossed. True love can happen in your 40's, and 50's too. Sometimes you meet and then separate.

Naina Khemani

Naina is a freelance creative content writer. She loves to read graphic novels and can spend her whole day being a couch potato. Reading so many graphic novels has created a whole new world inside her mind, and she has so many ideas that she can write on. She is that cringe GenZ, but also the kind of friend that everyone would want in their lives.

Vanshika Gupta

A postgraduate in economics and a writer by feels, Vanshika hails from the UT of Jammu and Kashmir, India. To find the calm to her storm, she started writing her heart out and so writing about everything that she felt at her core became her meditation. She think that words have a great power to inspire and heal and firmly believes in the idea of 'hoping against hope'.

Aniket Gauns

Aniket hails from Goa, a typical Goan guy who likes to balance work with leisure. He is a filmmaker by profession and likes to write rooted stories. Being an engineer by education, he has a keen interest in physics and new technologies. He believes that any story can move anyone at any time, so if you have the urge to write, you should.

Shay P. Kris

Digital Marketer, Chef, and now Poet and Author! It seems there is nothing Shay can't do. She usually writes when inspiration strikes her, and when it doesn't, she is researching what next to write on. In her spare time, she curls up on her sofa watching 90's sitcoms and watching over the cooking.

Shelina Rajawat

Shelina Rajawat is a 21-year-old, doing her Master's in clinical psychology and has her organization about mental health services called *'Therapy4us'*. She loves Italian food and wine. If she is not behind her laptop you will find her exploring the city and trying out seafood. She loves writing, has been part of various anthologies, and has her blog.

Prerna Dhingra

Prerna Dhingra is an Assistant Professor by profession and a budding writer by passion. She has been a hard-working postgraduate in English Literature, with a Diploma in Spanish to quench her thirst for exploration and creativity. She has also interned with The Indian Express and got five of her bylines published. Currently, she invests her time and energy as a civil servant aspirant. Enthusiastic about writing and changing the world through her pen, she is on a mission to be unstoppable.

Nadeem Shah

Nadeem Shah is a freelance journalist and an aspiring short story writer based in Srinagar, Kashmir.